A Gangster's Syn

**Lock Down Publications
and
Ca$h Presents**
A Gangster's Syn
A Novel by J-Blunt

A Gangsta's Syn

Lock Down Publications

P.O. Box 870494
Mesquite, Tx 75187

Visit our website

www.lockdownpublications.com

Lock Down Publications
Like our page on Facebook: Lock Down Publications @
www.facebook.com/lockdownpublications.ldp
Cover design and layout by: **Dynasty Cover Me**
Book interior design by: **Shawn Walker**
Edited by: **Lauren Burton**

Stay Connected with Us!

Text **LOCKDOWN** to 22828 to stay up-to-date with new releases, sneak peeks, contests and more...

Submission Guideline.

Submit the first three chapters of your completed manuscript to ldpsubmissions@gmail.com, subject line: Your book's title. The manuscript must be in a .doc file and sent as an attachment. The document should be in Times New Roman, double-spaced and in size 12 font. Also, provide your synopsis and full contact information. If sending multiple submissions, they must each be in a separate email.

Have a story but no way to send it electronically? You can still submit to LDP/Ca$h Presents. Send in the first three chapters, written or typed, of your completed manuscript to:

LDP: Submissions Dept
Po Box 870494
Mesquite, Tx 75187

DO NOT send original manuscript. Must be a duplicate.

Provide your synopsis and a cover letter containing your full contact information.

Thanks for considering LDP and Ca$h Presents.

Part 1: Genesis

J-Blunt

Chapter 1

"Don't worry, babe. Everything gon' be a'ight. They just trynna spook me by offering me only one deal. But they gotta come wit' anotha one 'cause they ain't got no hard evidence."

"So, how much longer until this is all over? We need you home, baby," Loretta asked, caressing the side of their three-month-old daughter's face.

"I asked for a speedy trial, and it's already been eight months. They got rules to this shit, but the courts is so backed up that it's taking longer. Hopefully another month or two and it'll be over."

Loretta tucked the phone between her shoulder and ear as she positioned the infant upon her breast and began patting her back. "I hope so. You missing so much of our daughter's life. She growin' bigger every day."

"I know. I stare at the pictures every night. I hate that I missed her birth. But when I come home, I'ma watch the video of it so much it's gon' feel like I was there."

"I just can't believe we have a daughter. I never–"

"Hey, baby. I gotta go. They lockin' down the unit and about to shut off the phones. I love–"

Click.

"No!" Loretta whined. She didn't even get to say bye.

After hanging up the phone, she began staring down at her daughter. She didn't know how she would take care of the little girl. She was twenty years old, broke, and barely had a firm grasp on life. And with the way things were looking, she would probably have to take care of her daughter by herself. Thoughts of her man never coming home sent a chill through her body. He was the love of her life. Her world. Her everything. And now he was gone, the possibility of him returning to the free world slim to none. She could feel the tears threatening to spill.

Just as a tear began to slide down her face, a key was being inserted into the lock on the front door. "Hey, girl," Rhoda called as she walked in the house. She was followed by her man, Rasheed.

"Hey, Rhoda. Hey, Sheed."

"'Sup, Loretta," Rasheed nodded as he walked toward the back of the house.

"What's wrong, girl? Did you and C-Money argue again?" Rhoda asked tenderly as she sat down on the couch and wrapped an arm around Loretta.

The tears fell freely. "No. I just miss him. It's tearing me apart that he locked up. He my world, Rhoda. I don't know what I'ma do if he don't come home soon. We don't even got nowhere to lay our heads at. I need him."

"It's okay, girl. You and li'l mama can stay with us as long as y'all need."

"Thanks. I don't know what I would do without y'all, Rhoda. I'ma pay y'all back as soon as C-Money come home."

"Psh! Girl, I don't care about no money. We like family. Plus, I know if Sheed got locked up, y'all would do the same thing for me."

"Yeah. You right. Thanks. I'ma go put li'l mama to bed and write C-Money a letter. That's my therapy."

After giving Rhoda a half-hug, Loretta got up from the pea-green sofa with her daughter tucked tightly in her arms and walked into the room Rhoda allowed her to stay in. The room housed all of her belongings: clothes, a bed, a crib, a radio, a TV, and hundreds of pictures of her and C-Money taped on the walls.

It hadn't always been like this. Eight months ago she

lived in a $350,000 house, drove a Mustang, and wore the finest clothes. All that changed when the FBI came. They took everything she couldn't prove wasn't bought with drug money. Everything. They even seized all of their bank accounts.

After laying her daughter in the crib, Loretta grabbed a notebook and pen and turned on the radio. Aaliyah sang about writing a four-page letter while Loretta wrote. In the letter, she expressed her ups and downs and her want for C-Money to be back home. Three hours, fourteen pages, and a hand cramp later, she decided to take a break. She needed to use the bathroom and get a snack.

The scent of weed hit her nostrils as soon as she opened the door. She didn't smoke, but she liked the smell of the funky aroma. As she passed Rhoda's room, her longing for C-Money was intensified. She could hear Rhoda and Rasheed laughing behind the closed door. She longed for moments like those with C-Money.

"You still woke?" Rhoda asked when Loretta walked out of the bathroom. She was digging through the fridge, dressed in a small, maroon robe that did a poor job of hiding all of her womaness. Rhoda was a big girl. Not fat, but country-thick and big-boned. She stood 5'9", was black as night, and had her shoulder-length permed hair wrapped up in a purple bandanna.

"Yeah. Just finished my letter. Need a little snack before I got to bed," Loretta said, bending next to Rhoda to search the fridge for something to eat.

"I picked up some pound cake this morning. Want some?"

"Ooh! You got that cherry stuff on top again?"

"And you know it! Sit down, girl. I'ma hook you up. So, how is it looking for C-Money?" Rhoda asked as she sat the cake on the table and went to get plates from the cabinet over the sink.

"I don't know. He say it's going good, but all I can think about is what the D.A. offered him. Sixty years to plead guilty. And that's only on the state charges. The Feds don't wanna deal until the state case is done."

"Damn. These white folks always takin' our men. So, how you holding up? You look stressed. Tense," Rhoda said as she gave Loretta a slice of the cake and went to put the rest back in the fridge.

"I am. My whole body is tight. I need a release. Wish I had some money to get a massage," Loretta commented as she dug into the dessert.

"Girl, I give the best massages. Put Rasheed ass to sleep every time." Without warning, Rhoda walked up behind Loretta and began massaging her shoulders.

Loretta closed her eyes and enjoyed the kneading of her friend's fingers. "Damn, Rhoda. That shit feels good!"

"Oh, yeah. You real tense. But I got you, girl."

"Damn. Rhoda! I need a massage, not a titty rub," Loretta cracked when she felt Rhoda's 34F's press into her head, neck, and back.

"Don't knock it 'til you try it," Rhoda quipped.

Loretta's eyes shot open. "Thanks for the massage and the cake. I gotta get back to my baby."

"Damn, Loretta. Why you trippin'?"

"Girl, you high. Fuck y'all been smoking?" Loretta said, looking Rhoda from head to toe as she stood.

"Loretta, wait. I helped you, now help me."

Even in the Goodwill jogging suit, Loretta looked good. Her light brown skin had a healthy glow, her hair long and curly. She had the face of a model and the body of a stripper, 34DD breasts, a small waist, and a booty that demanded attention.

"I know you ain't trynna go there with me?" Loretta asked, feeling her anger rise.

"It's just Sheed. He keep askin' me for a threesome. Can you–"

"I'm not gay, Rhoda. I like dick. And I'm not cheating on C-Money."

"But he's in jail and might not ever get out."

Loretta's face twisted into an angry mask. "Don't say that shit!" she shrieked, her eyes filling with tears.

"I'm sorry. I didn't mean it. It just came out."

"Don't say that shit, Rhoda. Don't say that shit."

"I swear I won't say it again. I'm sorry. But I need your help. I don't want no strange bitch in my house. I knew you since we were fourteen. I trust you."

"I can't do it, Rhoda. I can't."

"Yes, you can. Just once. Please."

Loretta mulled it over in her mind. She didn't want to do it, but she felt indebted to Rhoda and Rasheed for taking care of her and her baby. Anything she needed, they provided without hesitation. She knew she couldn't deny their request.

"Okay."

A devious smile spread across Rhoda's face. "C'mon."

***

"Look who still woke," Rhoda sang as she led Loretta into the bedroom she shared with Rasheed.

Rasheed was lying on the bed watching an X-rated movie. He was smoking a blunt. Naked. "'Sup, Loretta?" he smiled, blowing out a cloud of weed smoke.

"Hey," Loretta said sheepishly, looking around the room to avoid looking at Rasheed's nakedness.

Rasheed wasn't ugly. In fact, he was handsome in an Ice Cube sort of way. Brown skin, neatly trimmed afro, stocky build, nice teeth, and always wore a mean mug. Problem was, Loretta wasn't attracted to him, nor did she want to see him naked.

"Here. Hit this. Get comfortable," Rasheed said, offering Loretta the weed.

Loretta had only smoked weed a couple of times back in high school. She didn't care for mood-altering agents, but as she looked at Rasheed and Rhoda, she reached for the blunt. She knew she would need all the help she could get to get through the evening.

"Sit down, girl," Rhoda said, sitting down on the bed next to Rasheed.

Loretta did as she was told, taking a long drag on the blunt as she sat. When the smoke filled her lungs, she began choking.

Rasheed burst out laughing. "Damn, girl! Slow down. That's hydro. Can't be huffin' that like it's bunk."

When Loretta was finally able to get her cough under control, she could feel the weed high kick in. Her body began to vibrate, and she swore she could hear her heartbeat.

"Let me help you with this," Rhoda said, tugging at Loretta's sweatshirt.

Rasheed's eyes popped when Loretta's milk-engorged breasts were freed. They were big and firm and made his mouth water.

"Kiss her, baby," he encouraged Rhoda.

Loretta's eyes got as big as saucers. She didn't want to kiss another woman, let alone her best friend. Before she could protest, Rhoda's lip were upon hers. "Nun-un!" Loretta moved her head.

"Awe, c'mon, Loretta. Chill," Rasheed sulked.

"No. I'm not kissing no girls."

"A'ight, a'ight. I respect that. But show me what you would do wit' that cake, Rhoda," Rasheed said, looking at the cake Rhoda sat on the dresser.

Rhoda took his cue. She grabbed the cake and put some of the cherry topping on Loretta's nipples. When Rhoda's lips met her breasts, Loretta closed her eyes and lay back on the bed, allowing her friend to lick her breasts clean.

Not wanting the girls to have all the fun, Rasheed got up and walked around the bed. When he tugged at Loretta's jogging pants, she lifted her butt off the bed and allowed him to pull them off. When she was naked, he stood over her, admiring her curves. She looked just like he had imagined. And after he finished his inspection, he dove between her legs face-first.

Loretta didn't want to like his tongue. She tried to fight off the pleasures running through her body. She thought about fat people, clowns, and even old ladies, but nothing worked. It had been eight months since someone had been between her thighs, and Rasheed was no slouch with his tongue.

"Ooh!" she moaned, grabbing a fistful of the bedspread as Rasheed worked her clit while Rhoda worked her breasts. It only took a few minutes for her to cum.

"Damn, girl. You taste like Crème Savers!" Rasheed said, licking the cum off his lips as he crawled onto the bed. "Now, y'all come suck this big-ass dick!"

Chapter 2

"What's wrong, baby?" C-Money asked, looking at Loretta intently through the two-inch thick Plexiglas window.

"Nothing. I was thinking about your next court date. I want you to come home."

"You been wearin' this face every day for a week. Why you lyin' to me? We been together for three years. I know when you not tellin' me somethin'. So, what ain't you tellin' me?"

"It's nothing, babe. It's just hard for me. For us. The police took everything, and I'm worried about how I will take care of our daughter. I'm worried about you. What happens if—?"

"Don't think like that, baby. You gotta believe in me and have faith. Don't give up hope, and don't give up on me."

"I'm not. It's just hard."

"I know it's hard, but things will get better. Trust me."

"I trust you, baby," Loretta sighed.

"So, that's all you have to tell me?" C-Money asked, not letting her off the hook. She was hiding something. He knew it.

"Yes. Everything is fine."

C-Money studied her face for a few moments. He knew she was lying. Her body language had betrayed her. She kept fidgeting and wouldn't look him in his eyes. It hurt that she was hiding something from him. She had never done that before. After a few moments of staring, he decided to leave the issue alone. Things were hard enough for them, and he didn't want to add any stress to their situation. Whatever she was hiding, he knew it would come out. Eventually.

"My trial starts next week. They haven't come up with a good deal, so I'm goin' all the way."

Loretta's body language changed when he mentioned his court date. All her senses were alerted, and she kept eye contact. "But I thought you said they would come with a better deal? What happens if you lose at trial?"

"I ain't gon' lose, babe. They ain't got shit on me. They just trynna scare me. The state case is all circumstantial."

"I hope so. I miss your touch so much. I want you home. We need you," Loretta whined.

"I'll be home soon, I promise. Just–"

"Simmons! Visit's over!" a voice interrupted on the overhead intercom.

"Damn," C-Money moaned, his eyes becoming dark with sadness.

"I'll be back on your next visiting day. And call me later. I'll borrow another hundred from Rhoda," Loretta said, raising her palm to the glass.

C-Money did the same. "Okay. I'ma have T.O. drop you off a couple hundred. I love you."

"I love you, too."

***

During the drive back to Rhoda's house, Loretta's conscience ate at her. It had been this way since her threesome with Rhoda and Rasheed, and now she was sure C-Money knew of her indiscretion. She had never lied to him, and the first time she had done it, her body betrayed her. She knew if he found out she cheated on him, it would crush him and add to his already full plate of stress.

By the time she got back to Rhoda's, she had narrowed her options down to two choices: become a better liar or tell C-Money the truth. As she entered the house, she recited the next lie in her mind. She knew she had to be ready, just in case.

"So, how was your visit?" Rhoda asked as soon as Loretta closed the door.

"Any time I get to be with him is a blessing. Thanks for letting me use your car again. And for watching li'l mama," Loretta said as she handed Rhoda the car keys.

"No problem. All she do is sleep. But I gotta get to work. I'ma see you later. If Rasheed come home, tell him to answer his beeper."

"Okay."

Five minutes after Rhoda left, Loretta heard a key being inserted into the lock on the front door. "'Sup, Loretta?" Rasheed asked as he walked into the house.

"Rhoda been paging you. She said call her back." Loretta said dryly as she picked up her sleeping daughter and walked toward her room. She hated being around Rasheed when Rhoda wasn't home.

"Hey! Hold on! Where you goin'?" Rasheed called, following behind her.

"What do you want, Rasheed?" Loretta asked as she lay her daughter in the crib.

"I wanna know how you doin'. See how my nigga C-Money holdin' up."

"I'm good, and he good. Just trynna make it."

"So, y'all don't need nothin'? C-Money was a good nigga, and I fuck wit' good dudes," Rasheed said, pulling a wad of cash from the front pocket of his designer jeans.

Loretta seen through his attempt at being a good guy. "What do you really want, Rasheed?"

Rasheed paused for a moment, letting his cash-filled hands fall to his side. "I want some more of that good-ass pussy. I want you to be my side bitch."

Loretta looked at him like he was wearing clothes

washed in garbage juice. "Nigga, is you crazy? I told y'all that was a one-time thing. My friend loves you, Sheed. I can't do her like that. And I'm not cheating on my man again."

"This ain't 'bout Rhoda or C-Money. This 'bout me and you. You gimme what I want and I'ma give you what you need. I can upgrade you, ma. Don't you want yo' own shit again? Ain't you tired of beggin' and borrowin'?" Rasheed asked, throwing a stack of fifty-dollar bills on the bed.

"I don't care about your money, Rasheed. I love my man. And my friend. I'm not doing this," Loretta said, picking up the money from the bed and holding it out to him.

Rasheed refused to take the money. "Well, I'ma tell you like this. You and yo' baby ain't cheap. Y'all spendin' my money and livin' in my house. All this shit is in my name. Either you get wit' the program or find you a homeless shelter."

Loretta's eyes began to fill with tears. She couldn't believe Rasheed was doing this to her. What was even more unbelievable was the thought of living in a homeless shelter. "Rasheed, you gon' do me and my baby like that if I don't give you some pussy?"

"I'm sayin', ma, I got needs. You and baby girl ain't cheap."

The room became silent. Loretta knew she couldn't take her daughter to a homeless shelter. She didn't even have a ride to get there if she chose to go. "What do you want me to do?"

Rasheed's eyes lit up. "For starters, you can throw that money back on the bed. That's you. I told you I gotchu. Then I'ma need you to put yo' lips on this dick." Rasheed pulled off his pants and lay on top of the pile of money.

After a little hesitation, Loretta knelt between his legs

and began to orally please him.

"Yeah, Loretta. Suck this dick. You my bitch now," Rasheed moaned, using his hand to guide her bobbing head. After a few minutes, he got tired of her mouth. "A'ight. That's enough. Take them jeans off, girl."

Loretta stood up and did as she was told. She hated Rasheed for making her have sex with him. Hated him so much she began to cry.

"Dry them tears, girl. Face down, ass up."

Loretta cut her eyes at him as she assumed the position.

"Awe, shit! Damn, C-money was a lucky-ass nigga," Rasheed moaned as he slid deep into her.

"Stop sayin' his name," Loretta grimaced.

Rasheed laughed. "Fuck you gon' do? Tell him? This my pussy now. You my bitch," Rasheed said, slapping her butt cheeks as he deep-stroked her.

Loretta didn't say another word. She knew it was no use. Rasheed had her right where he wanted her, and until she found out what would happen to C-Money, she needed Rasheed, Rhoda, and their charity.

"Say my name," Rasheed moaned, picking up his pace as he slapped her on the ass again.

Loretta didn't speak, grunt, or moan.

"Say my name, bitch!" Rasheed demanded, getting rough.

"Rasheed, you're hurting me," Loretta whined as she scooted across the bed, trying to get away from Rasheed's punishment.

Instead of letting up, he went harder and got rougher. Her whining had turned him on.

Loretta continued to inch and crawl across the bed, trying to get away from Rasheed's pounding. The more she wiggled, the harder he went. They eventually ended up pressed up against the wall. Loretta had run out of running room.

"Ain't no more runnin' now. Take this dick, bitch!"

Chapter 3

"Don't come to my verdict reading tomorrow."

"What? Why? I been at all your court dates. I sat through the whole trial. I think you can beat the murder. They don't got nothin' but a bunch of snitches. And J-Sun already admitted to killing him."

"I know that. And them people know that, too. They trynna say I ordered the hit. I think they gon' catch me up on that. So, stay home. You don't need to suffer through this shit no more."

"No, C-Money. I been here since the beginning, and I'm not going nowhere."

"Loretta, no! Don't come. Don't chu see what they trynna do? They ain't finna let me out. All them niggas that used to run wit' me testified on me. It's over, babe. They fucked me."

"No, Chris! Don't fuckin' say that!" Loretta screamed. "What happened to not giving up? What happened to keeping the faith and staying strong? I believed in you, baby. I can't live without you. The baby needs you. I need you."

"We ran outta hope and our faith dried up. We gotta face reality, ma. It don't matter who or what we believe in. Can't nothin' change what happened at trial. They got me. It's over."

Loretta couldn't believe the dejection she was seeing in her man's eyes. It was foreign. Something she had never seen before. C-Money was the man on the streets. He exuded power and confidence. He seemed untouchable. He had been her rock. She believed in him because he believed in himself, but the look on his face and the tears that threatened to spill from his eyes told her he had given up. He had lost hope. His circumstances had changed his vision.

"What are we gonna do? What do you need me to do? Do you need a new lawyer? Can we appeal?" Loretta asked, refusing to throw in the towel.

"I need you to forget about me and move on wit' yo' life. Don't let our daughter know where I am. I'ma die in here, and you gon' die, too, if you stay wit' me."

"I don't care about that, Chris. I don't care how long they give you. We won't leave you. I can't."

"Forget me, Loretta. Please, babe. I'ma suffer if I know I'm hurting you. You only twenty. I'm thirty-five. I lived. I seen the world. I did it all. If you stay wit' me, I'ma hold you back. You too beautiful and smart to be stuck wit' a nigga doin' time. I told you I seen yo' potential when I first laid eyes on you. That's why I took you under my wings even though you was seventeen. Use what you learned from me and live."

"No, Chris. I'm not leaving."

C-Money exploded. "*Leave*, Loretta! I'm not comin' home!"

"No, no, no, no!"

"Simmons! You and you visitor are disturbing the rest of the visitors. Your visit has been terminated," a voice yelled over the intercom.

Loretta and C-Money stared at each other intently. "Don't come to my court date tomorrow."

***

"Relax, girl. It's gon' be alright," Rhoda said, reaching over and patting Loretta's thigh.

Loretta continued staring out the windshield, gnawing at her fingernails. "He didn't call me last night. Something is wrong. I can feel it."

"Well, we about to see him now. Hopefully they will let us visit him afterwards."

"Yeah. Hopefully," Loretta sighed.

After parking in the county parking lot, Loretta and Rhoda made the trek to the courthouse. Both of their nerves were fried, and they had the jitters. Once they were inside, it didn't take them long to find the courtroom they were looking for: Branch 25, presided over by the Honorable Judge Ronald Franks. When they opened the door to enter the court's viewing area, they were surprised at what they seen. The rows and pews were packed. Hundreds of people were stuffed into the seats, including the media, a sea of policemen and women, and C-Money's family and friends.

Loretta didn't bother going over to sit with his family. After he got locked up, they acted like they didn't know her. They wouldn't even help her with the baby, so her and Rhoda found a seat next to one of the many news coverage teams.

"Ugh! They over there actin' like they shit don't stank," Rhoda spat, rolling her eyes at C-Money's family.

"Not today, Rhoda. I don't have the energy to deal with them."

"I hope you don't ever let them see li'l mama. Bitches act like they don't know you now that C-Money locked up. They so fake."

"I'll raise my baby by myself before I ever ask them–"

Loretta was cut off by a commotion that stirred the pews. Video cameras recorded, cameras flashed, and the police booed as a door at the back of the courtroom opened and C-Money was escorted by bailiffs to a seat next to his lawyers.

C-Money's complexion was high yellow. He was bi-racial, black and white. He stood 6'5" and weighed a little over 200 pounds. His hair was freshly cut into a neat afro and his facial hair was trimmed. The tailored blue suit he wore made him look more like a CEO than a man on trial for murder.

Loretta ignored the commotion. Seeing her man made her pulse quicken as a huge smile spread across her face. But he didn't even notice her. He wasn't expecting to see her, so instead of acknowledging her presence, he smiled and waved at his family.

"Look at that motherfucker smiling," one of the police officers mumbled from somewhere behind Loretta.

"I wish we had the death penalty. I would love to see his ass fry," another commented.

"All rise!" the courtroom bailiff called.

A hush passed over the viewing area as Judge Franks positioned himself behind the bench. He was a tall white man in his mid-60s. He had a slender frame and wore his salt-and-pepper hair in a comb-over.

"You may be seated," he called as he took the bench.

Feet shuffled as everyone sat.

"We are gathered here on this fourth day of September in the year 1995 in the matter of Christopher Simmons versus the state of Wisconsin. The charge: first-degree intentional homicide of a peace officer, party to a crime. All parties are present and ready to receive the verdict," a female court reporter announced.

"Please bring in the jury," Judge Franks told his bailiff.

The brown-skinned courtroom officer walked across the room and to a side door. He walked in and came out a few moments later with the jury in tow: eight men, four women, all of them white.

"Mr. Foreman, has the jury reached a verdict?" Judge Franks asked after the jury was seated.

A graying white man in a tan suit stood to his feet. "Yes,

sir. We have."

"What say you?"

"Your Honor, we, the jury, find Christopher Simmons, the defendant, guilty of–"

Gasps and cheers filled the pews, forcing the foreman to halt his recitation of the verdict.

C-Money hung his head.

Loretta began to sob.

"Quiet down, people! Order in the court!" the judge yelled, banging his gavel. "I have allowed you all into my courtroom, and I demand you honor these proceedings. Any more outbursts will not be tolerated, and you will be kicked out, fined, or held in contempt. You have been warned. Now, Mr. Foreman, what is your verdict?"

"Your Honor, we, the jury, find the defendant guilty of first degree intentional homicide of Peace Officer Hector Martinez."

"Thank you, sir. The jury is excused."

While the bailiff escorted the jury from the room, the judge turned to C-Money.

"Mr. Simmons, a jury of your peers has convicted you of first degree intentional homicide in the murder of a peace officer. You–"

"Them ain't my mu'fuckin' peers!" C-Money yelled.

While Judge Franks stared down at C-Money with the meanest look he could muster, C-Money's lawyers grabbed at him, trying to cover his mouth.

"Mr. Simmons, we will continue these proceedings with or without you. Am I clear?"

"Fuck you, Judge Franks! You pink-ass bitch! I'ma fuck you up!" C-Money yelled, struggling to free himself from his lawyers.

"Remove him from my court!" the judge yelled, turning

beet red.

That's when all hell broke loose. Three bailiffs rushed over to detain C-Money. He managed to punch one of them in the mouth before the other two tackled him to the ground. Gasps filled the pews as everyone stood to their feet to get a better view. Loretta was front and center. She watched as the three tactically trained officers wrestled with C-Money. Every time they thought they had him pinned, he broke free. He got the upper hand when he grabbed one of the bailiff's guns and shot him in the leg.

"He's got a gun! He's got a gun!" One of the police officers yelled from the pews.

While everyone in the viewing area trampled one another to get out of the courtroom, Loretta continued to stand, transfixed by the scene playing out before her. She watched through wide eyes as C-Money turned and shot a bailiff that was trying to run for cover. He spun to shoot the other bailiff, but missed as he ducked into a side room.

C-Money spun around, looking for someone else to shoot. His eyes stopped at the judge's seat. Franks had already ducked for cover. Several police from the viewing area charged into the courtroom, guns drawn. When C-money noticed the movement, he spun to face them, ready to shoot.

And that's when he seen Loretta.

"I thought I told you not to–"

Pop-pop-pop-pop-pop-pop-pop-pop-pop-pop-pop-pop!

Chapter 4

Knock, knock, knock, knock.

"What?" Loretta called, keeping her head under the blanket.

"Can I come in?" Rhoda asked, leaning against the door.

"Why?"

"Because I'm worried about you," Rhoda said, peeking her head into the room.

"I'm good. I just want to be alone."

Rhoda ignored her friend's want and sat on the bed. "But you been in this room for a week. You're depressed. You need to get out."

"I don't want to go out. I want to be left alone."

"Well, I'm about to go to work. Do you need anything? Does li'l mama need Pampers?"

"No."

"Loretta?" Rhoda called, wanting to see her face.

"What?"

"Loretta?"

"What, Rhoda? What?"

"Can you just look at me?"

Loretta flung the cover from her face. The heavy bags were still fresh under her eyes. "What?"

"I'm worried about you, girl. You been eating? Sleeping?"

"I can't eat. My food won't stay down. And I don't have an appetite. And I can't sleep. I'm scared to close my eyes. I keep seeing them kill him."

"Do you want to see a doctor or a psychologist? Is there anything we can do?"

"No. I just want to be left alone. Please." Loretta said before pulling the blanket back over her head.

Rhoda wanted to say more. She was really worried about her friend, but the way Loretta was acting let Rhoda know the best medicine was probably for her to leave Loretta alone. "Well, I'm about to leave. Call me if you need anything."

When Loretta heard the front door close, she brought her head from under the blanket. Her eyes roamed over the pictures of her and C-Money taped on the walls. Memories of their life flooded her mind. How they met, all the trips, the day she told him she was pregnant. Those were some of the happiest moments of her life. Remembering the good old days made her smile.

Then C-Money's bullet riddled body forced itself into her thoughts, turning her smile into a frown. She couldn't believe he was gone. Couldn't believe he would never get to meet their daughter.

Then, as if on cue, the baby stirred. She let out a small cry, then the small cry turned into a big one.

"Okay, okay," Loretta groaned as she climbed out of the bed and walked over to the crib. She reached down to pick up the crying baby. After sitting on the bed, she checked her diaper. It was soiled. "Okay, little lady. Momma gonna get you all cleaned up. Yes, she is."

After changing her diaper, Loretta sat the infant in her car seat and went to fix a bottle. She had just finished making the milk when the front door opened.

"You finally decided to get out of bed, huh?" Rasheed commented as he walked into the kitchen.

"Hey, Sheed," Loretta said dryly, moving quickly to put away everything she used to make the bottle. She wanted to get away from him as fast as she could.

"You sound real happy to see me," he said sarcastically, tossing a Gucci tote onto the kitchen table.

"Not now, Sheed. I just want to be left alone," Loretta said, grabbing the bottle and heading for her room.

Rasheed grabbed her arm, stopping her from leaving. "Wait. Where you goin'?"

"Rasheed, stop! Leave me alone!" Loretta yelled, trying to wrestle her arm away.

Rasheed pulled her into him, wrapping his arm around her waist. "So, that's how you talk to yo' nigga?"

"Let me go, Sheed!"

"Girl, stop! I want some pussy. That nigga dead. He left yo' ass. I'm all you and that li'l girl got."

"Watch yo' mouth! And let me go!" Loretta yelled, biting him on the shoulder.

"Ah, shit, bitch!" Rasheed yelled, picking her up and throwing her across the kitchen. Loretta collided with the kitchen table, the milk bottle flying from her hand as the Gucci tote fell onto the floor. A sea of hundred-dollar bills spilled out.

"You gon' pay for that shit!" Rasheed said, rubbing the stinging bite mark.

"Rasheed, stop! Just leave me, alone," Loretta cried, backpedaling as Rasheed approached her.

"You my bitch now. When I say fuck me, you s'posed to fuck me. C-Money ain't comin' back. You ain't got nobody but me."

"Don't say his fuckin' name no more," Loretta growled, her anger rising and fear disappearing.

"Or what? Fuck you gon' do, bitch?"

"Fuck you!" Loretta screamed as she charged at him.

Rasheed dodged her wild punches and delivered one of his own. It landed on her throat, making it hard for her to breathe. While she struggled to catch her breath, Rasheed picked her up and threw her against the sink.

"Now, I said gimme some pussy, bitch," he demanded, bending her over and pulling her sweatpants down. He had just freed himself from his boxers when Loretta spun around with a steak knife she had grabbed from the sink.

"Ah, shit!" Rasheed yelled, grabbing the right side of his chest where Loretta had stabbed him. He stumbled backward and looked at the blood.

When Loretta seen the shock and fear in his eyes, it excited her. She remembered all the times he forced himself upon her. All the times he called her a bitch. She hated him. Hated him almost as much as she hated the police who killed C-Money. And when she thought about how bad he talked about C-Money, she snapped. She ran at him with the knife and stabbed him until he stopped moving.

"Oh, my God! Oh, my God!" Loretta panicked when she came to her senses. She had just killed her friend's boyfriend. "Oh, shit! Oh, shit!" she groaned as she began to hyperventilate. She took deep breaths and paced the kitchen, trying to think of her next move.

The sound of her daughter's cries brought her back from the trance. She knew she had to leave. Run away. If the police caught her, they would lock her up and take her baby. She couldn't allow that to happen.

She ignored the dead man's look on Rasheed's face as she searched his pockets. After she found the keys to his BMW, she grabbed the Gucci tote full of money and went to get her daughter.

Part 2: The New Testament

J-Blunt

Chapter 5

"Oh, shit! Damn!"

I loved getting my pussy ate. If I had to choose between a big dick and a wet tongue, I would be dickless for the rest of my life. And right now, Ferrary was validating my hypothetical choice.

"Yeah. Right there. Right there!" I moaned, grabbing two fistfuls of her hair as she worked the four-inch dildo in my hole while she sucked my clit. She definitely knew what she was doing.

"Oh, yeah! Damn, baby girl!" She was sucking me hard, and I could feel my insides bubbling. I was about to cum. It had been a week since my last orgasm, so I knew this one was about to be big.

"Ah! Oh, God! Oh, God!" I came long and hard. And it was messy.

"And that's why you should hire me," Ferrary said, licking my juices from her lips as she got up from her knees.

For a few moments I was speechless. The orgasm had taken my breath. "Girl, for head like that, I'm thinking about making you a manager," I laughed.

I didn't normally sleep around with my staff. I hated mixing business with pleasure because a scorned lover could ruin a business, but when this nineteen-year-old stallion walked into my office and offered to show me why she would make a good employee, I made an exception to my rule. The bonus was that Ferrary was finer than fine. I mean movie star gorgeous. The thing was, she didn't know her worth. She was young and dumb. I had been that way once. A long time ago.

"So, when do I start?" she asked with a giggle.

Ferrary looked like a schoolgirl, like she had literally left school on her lunch break and come to me for a job. She still had that twinkle in her eyes. An innocent look. A baby face with a grown woman's body.

"You just did. And you're definitely starting off on the right foot. Or should I say knee?" I smiled, giving her a wink as I got up from the couch and went over to my desk. I went into the drawer and grabbed a contract. "You look over this while I go freshen up. And your next job is to clean off that couch for me. There are some cleaning supplies in the closet."

After excusing myself, I went to the bathroom at the back of my office to take a quick shower. When I came out of the bathroom, I was pleased to see my black leather couch clean of the cum stain and the signed contract sitting on my desk. "So, are you sure you want to do this?" I asked after sitting at my desk and looking over the contract.

"I really need the money, Syncere. I don't got nobody looking out for me."

"Well, I'm going to fit you in three nights a week for now. Once you get some time in, you'll be a regular. Did you read the rules?"

"Yes."

"Good. And just because you sucked my pussy don't mean I'ma show you favoritism. This is a job, Ferrary. While you're in my place, you will act professionally. Clear?" I asked, letting her know to separate business from pleasure. I had to erase the possibility of her getting bigheaded because she made me cum.

"Yes. I understand. I won't let you down."

Time would tell. I had heard lots of promises. Experience told me they were meant to be broken. "Okay. Well, come back tomorrow night. 11:00 P.M."

"Okay. Thank you so much, Syncere. Thank you,"

Ferrary beamed, standing to shake my hand.

"Don't trip, girl. You earned it."

After the handshake, I watched her bubble butt jiggle in the black spandex as she left my office. She had the kind of ass that made other women go and get injections. Round, plump, and firm. For a moment I thought about calling her back into my office and stretching her out with my ten-inch strap-on. I eventually decided against it. I didn't want her to get attached.

I was filing her contract in my desk when there was a knock on my door. "Come in."

"Hey, Syn. I need to give you this," Jaki said as she walked into my office. Jaki was one of my first employees. She was dark-skinned and 5'4" with crazy curves. She had been with me for a little over a year.

"How much?" I asked as I counted the roll of bills she gave me."

"Eight bills."

"Okay," I confirmed after my count. I went into my drawer and pulled out my receipt book to record the transaction. When done, I gave her a copy.

"Thanks."

"No problem. You know I take care of my girls," I winked. And I meant that. I would go to bat for any of the women who worked for me. I was all for girl power. The trials in my life turned me into a feminist of sorts. I was serious about women's suffrage and women's rights. I helped the cause by being a bank for the girls who needed it. I saved some of their money for them. And I kept receipts. All the money the girls gave me, I invested. So it grew. A lot. And whenever they needed some help, I gave them their investment with a little bit of interest.

When Jaki left my office, I lotioned up and dressed in a

purple Prada pantsuit. Time was money, and I had business to attend to.

***

"Miss Evans! Welcome," Travis Kratz greeted me, smiling wide.

Travis was my accountant. I hooked up with him a little over a year ago. I had heard of him through word of mouth and done my homework. Word was he was the guy who could make old money look new, and they were right. He turned my dirty $100,000 into a clean $85,000. I took $50K to start my business and invested $35K. A year later, both were turning profits.

"Hey, Travis," I purred, giving his outstretched hand a shake before sitting down in the chair in front of his desk.

"Glad you could come by," he smiled, showing his pearly whites. Travis was a good-looking man. He had that Terrance Howard thing going on. He was high yellow, had light brown eyes, a small, neatly packed afro, and often wore his facial hair trimmed up with a 5 o'clock shadow. He stood about 6'6", and even though I hadn't seen his body, I knew it was as finely tuned as a new BMW. I had thought about seducing him on countless occasions. But I didn't. I didn't want to mix business with pleasure.

"No problem. What's up?"

"There is something I need to tell you, Miss Evans." His tone was serious. Like somebody was about to die.

"Okay."

"I'm going to be leaving Marty and Sloan. I got a promotion. To Goldman Sachs. In New York."

"Oh," I managed.

"Yeah. It just kinda came out of the blue. I mean, I put in

an application over two months ago. I never expected them to call, but they did. I start in two weeks."

"Okay," I mumbled. I wanted to be happy for him. I really did. But I wasn't. All I could think about was my money. Travis had pulled a lot of strings for me, had turned my five digits into six. I trusted him and didn't want to see him go.

"Hey, you don't have to look all sad. The world is not over."

"I know. I'm happy for you, Travis. I am. But I can't help but think of myself. I need your help. Your advice."

"Hey, c'mon, Syncere. You know I wouldn't leave you hanging. I got somebody who will take good care of you. He's on vacation now, but as soon as he returns, I'll introduce you to him. He's a good guy. Young, street-smart, and motivated. Kind of reminds me of me," he smiled smugly.

I rolled my eyes. "We'll see." I liked his confidence in the new guy, but I still didn't like putting my money in a stranger's hands.

"Has anybody ever told you that you look sexy when you're mad?" he flirted.

I gave him a sassy look as I stood to my feet. "I've heard that a time or two. Bye, Travis."

***

After leaving the accounting firm, I hopped in my black two-seater Nissan 3502. I had one more stop to make before I headed back to my club. I was always nervous when I made this trip, but I knew I had to make it. I looked over at the yellow envelope on my passenger seat as I turned onto 17th and Scott. My plan was to drop it in the mailbox and leave.

I drove slowly down the block, watching for anything or anyone who looked suspicious. If something looked out of whack, I would make the drop another time. I knew I was taking a huge risk doing this, but I had to. I didn't trust anyone enough to delegate this task. I had learned to keep my business to myself. I'd seen women use other women's secrets, weaknesses, and faults against them. So, for those reasons, I handled my own business, playing people and circumstances like chess. Always getting the checkmate, even if it meant making sacrifices. Like I was now. Risking my comfortable life to take care of something from my past.

After parking in front of a blue-and-gray one-story home, I checked the block again and both sides of the street. The coast looked clear. I grabbed the envelope from my passenger seat as I left my Nissan. I quick-stepped onto the sidewalk and upon the porch. I opened the small mailbox and dropped the envelope inside.

I was about to turn and leave when the door swung open.

Fuck.

"Who is you?"

I looked up and seen a tall, dark-skinned man standing in the doorway. He looked to be in his early twenties, wore his hair in cornrows to the back, and had on an oversized, dark t-shirt with baggy jeans.

"Oh. Hey. I was looking for Tanisha. She here?" I asked, thinking fast on my feet.

"Don't no Tanisha live here."

"Oh. Sorry. Damn GPS," I said as I backed away from the door.

"Who is it, A.J.?" a female voice called from inside the house.

Hearing her voice forced me to pause. Even though I had never heard the voice, I knew who it belonged to.

"Some lady. Said she got the wrong house."

I stared at him, memorizing every line of his face. Just in case.

"'Sup?" he asked after he caught me staring.

"Oh. Nothing. Sorry. Bye."

I spun on my heels and damn near sprinted to my car. I didn't know where the tears came from, but they threatened to spill from my eyes as I pulled away from the curb. "Get ahold of yourself, Syn. You are stronger than this. Pull it together." I told myself as I stared in the mirror at my light brown eyes. I hadn't cried in years, but hearing her voice had almost caused a flood.

Fuck.

I hated emotions. They complicated everything.

I grabbed my remote to my radio and found a song to help get my emotions under control. 2-Pac's *Ambitions of a Rider* brought my car's speakers to life.

By the time I pulled up to my club, I had my game face on. No more tears. Syn was back.

Chapter 6

"Oh, yes, Luke! Fuck me good, baby! I been a bad bitch. I'm a bad bitch!" Nya screamed as I long-stroked her.

Nya was one of my main freaks, and freak was putting it lightly. Nya was Nasty with a capital N. And I loved it. She wanted it in the mouth, pussy, and third eye at the same time. Her ultimate fantasy was to suck two dicks. Together. At the same time. Crazy shit. Extreme shit. Shit I wasn't down with. A bun has room for only one hot dog.

"Put it in my dookey, Lukey. Fuck my ass!" she demanded.

Who was I to deny her? Nya had one of the biggest and roundest asses I had ever seen. I loved hitting it from the back and watching it jiggle.

When she spun around and got on her knees, I gripped her ass cheeks, exposing her sphincter. I wasted no time going in.

"Ooh, shit!" she moaned as I slid in.

"You ready for Givenchy, bitch?" Nya liked when I talked rough to her. Straight-up freak!

"You ain't shit, nigga! Fuck you," she yelled, reaching back and scratching me across my stomach.

Oh, yeah! "Bitch!" I yelled, grabbing a handful of her bob as I pulled most of Givenchy out. I shoved my meat back into her ass with so much force I thought I would rupture her anal walls.

"Oh, shit! Yes, Luke. Mm!"

I rammed her unmercifully. I was stroking her so hard and fast that the small beads of sweat rolling down my back turned into what seemed like a shower. Every time my pelvis met her cheeks, it sounded like someone was being brutally beaten. And she loved it.

"Oh, shit! Fuck, yeah!" she yelled, throwing her ass back at me. "I'm 'bout to cum, Luke! I'm 'bout to cum!" she screamed.

I wasn't sure if we had neighbors in the hotel room next to us, but if we did, I knew they were either extremely pissed off or extremely turned on. And they definitely knew my name!

"Cum, bitch! You nasty, filthy, ho-bitch. Cum!"

"Ooh! Ah!" she screamed as she came.

I wasn't ready to bust my nut yet, but when she squeezed her anal muscles, I exploded. "Ah, shit! Damn, bitch! Damn!" I moaned as Givenchy coughed up semen. My release felt so good that the bottom of my feet tingled like I was about to have a stroke. "Damn, Nya. Where you learn that shit at?" I asked as I collapsed on the bed next to her.

"You know I keep my sex room poppin', Luke."

"Yeah, that shit was definitely poppin'. Definitely," I said as I sat up in bed.

"Wait. Where you goin'?" she asked, sounding like she wasn't done with me.

"You left a stain on me. Gotta clean it off."

I wasn't in the shower but two minutes when I heard footsteps on the bathroom floor. The cream shower curtain whipped open, and there stood Nya. All 5'2" and 135 pounds of her curvaceous body. She was looking at my soaped-up flesh like I was a Fruit Roll-up and she was a fat kid.

"I love shower sex," she purred.

So did I!

***

I woke up the next morning with my limbs tangled up in Nya's. I reached over and grabbed my phone from the bedside table to check the time. 7:08. Time to get ready.

After peeling my body away from Nya's, I headed to the shower. I had an important meeting in a little over an hour. A meeting so important I had jumped on an airplane and flown over two states to keep. A meeting I had made several times over the past six years. A meeting I would continue making for the rest of my life. Or his.

"Hey, I'm about to go," I told Nya when I walked back into the room.

"It's morning already?" she asked groggily. She was lying on her stomach, and when she stretched, she arched her back, making her enormous booty look even bigger. It made me want to jump back in that bed.

"Yep. Morning time. Rise and shine," I said as I slid into my boxers and Billionaire Mafia button-up shirt. After slipping on a pair of Billionaire Mafia jeans and my Creative Recreation shoes, I went back to the bathroom to give myself the once-over in the mirror. My brushed waves looked like the ocean, my mug was trimmed perfectly, and my skin, which I took good care of, had a healthy glow. In my line of work, appearance mattered. A lot. It could make or break a man, so I got my facial hair trimmed every two days, hair cut every week, and kept my nails trimmed, cleaned, and clear polished. I wasn't a metrosexual, but I definitely took care of myself.

"Damn, Luke! If you didn't have to leave..." Nya said, biting her bottom lip as I walked out of the bathroom.

I liked Nya. Not enough to wife, but I was definitely keeping her around. She was a natural beauty and wore very little make-up. Her Dominican roots gave her an exotic look. And she was a professional woman. A 27-year-old, educated, up-and-coming real estate agent. A good catch for somebody else.

"See if you be talkin' like that when I get back," I said as I bent to kiss her on the cheek.

"Don't tempt me."

"See you in a couple hours," I laughed, grabbing my Orisue coat from the closet before leaving the room.

After descending a flight of stairs, I left the Motel 6's lobby and stepped out into the Midwest's late spring/early summer morning. I strolled coolly toward the rented silver GTO, enjoying the light breeze that blew. I had already started the car before I left the room thanks to the automatic start, so after popping the locks and sticking the key in the ignition, I was off.

My destination was only twenty minutes away from the motel: the Terre Haute Maximum Security Prison in Terre Haute, Indiana. I hated prisons with a passion. They had been robbing black families of our brothers, fathers, uncles, and sons since their inception. And it was no secret my black brothers and sisters greatly outnumbered the masses of guilty and innocent people who filled cells all over the nation. Some of our best and brightest would never see the free world again. It was sad.

After driving into the gated fortress, I found a parking spot and joined the growing crowd of loved ones who came to show their love and support to the incarcerated. We stood outside the twenty-foot wire fence topped with razor wire. When the gate was opened, we walked through and into the world of the damned.

After I was IDed, searched, and questioned, I was allowed to enter into the visiting room. I had been here almost a hundred times, but every time I walking in, it seemed brand new.

When I found my table, I had a seat and began my wait. I don't know how long I was seated because in prison, time stands still. But I felt an unspeakable joy when I seen him.

"Luke! What's poppin', li'l bro?" my big brother, Barron "Big Chief" Swanson called across the visiting room.

"Big Bro!" I smiled as I stood to my feet.

Barron had been locked up for eight years, since I was nineteen. Terre Haute had been his home for the last six. According to the Feds, he was never getting out. Under the RICO Act, he had been given life. For me, that was unthinkable. Evil. Cruel and unusual punishment. Especially since he hadn't killed anyone.

"Look at chu, boy. I see some of my taste rubbed off on you," he said, giving my clothing an approving once-over.

"You jocking my swag, huh?" I smiled, striking a pose.

We burst out laughing.

"So, how is the family? Mom? Pop? Latia?" he asked as we sat across from each other at the small table.

"Everybody good, man. Gettin' older. You know how it is. Mom and Pop still keepin' on. I think Pop 'bout to retire in a couple of years."

"'Bout time. He pushin' 65. He should've been fell back into retirement."

"You know Pop. He want to work until he can't move," I laughed. It was true. Our father believed in working until he couldn't. He taught us the same thing. Preached it to us while growing up.

"I'ma call them sometime this week. It's been awhile," Barron said, drifting off.

Awhile was an understatement. Barron hadn't spoken to Mom and Pop in years. Before they stopped talking, every time he talked to Dad, they argued. Pop couldn't stop throwing Barron's life sentence in his face, and every time he talked to Mom, she preached Jesus. When Barron embraced Islam, she blew a fuse. Somewhere along the line he figured it would be easier to do his time without talking to them. Pop let go easily. Mom held on for a few years, up until Barron denied her visits. Now they exchanged cards on special occasions.

"Yeah. That would be cool. You know Mom want to talk to you."

"Yeah. I'ma call the old lady. I miss her. So, how is Latia?"

"She good. Seven going on seventeen," I laughed.

"When you get a minute, send me some up-to-date pictures. That's one thing I regret, Luke. Not having kids. I wish I could have left a piece of me out there."

"You gon' get another shot, bro. I know this ain't gon' be your home forever."

"I like yo' optimism, Luke, but these feds ain't no joke. They bury us real niggas in here because we refuse to snitch. If I woulda told on my plug, I probably would've only got ten to fifteen for those bricks. But my name means more than anything. The streets know Big Chief is a real nigga. I'ma take my lumps, li'l bro. Even if I never see the streets again."

***

After I left the prison, I got into the rental car and began replaying my visit with my brother. I found it both odd and honorable to take a life bid knowing he could have changed the outcome by giving the feds a bigger fish. Barron's choice taught me principles are not only quoted, but real men live and die by them.

As I pulled out of the parking lot, I wished like I did every time I left that I could take him with me. I hated that I got to leave and he had to stay. Sometimes I wished I could trade places with him, but I knew it was only a wish because

I didn't think I would last a single day in prison. I wasn't built for that life. I had dodged the streets and their pitfalls thanks to Barron.

J-Blunt

Chapter 7

"So, how is your brother doing? I haven't heard from him in a while."

"He good, Mom. Still keeping up his fight for freedom. He says hi to you and Pop."

"So, is he still 'practicing Islam'?" Mom asked, throwing up air quotes.

I smiled and shook my head. Mom was a high school teacher, had been for twenty years, and that was her politically correct side-talking. "Yeah, he still a Muslim, Mom. But that's not important. What's important is he is your son and he sends his love."

"That is important, Luke. His soul is on the line."

"C'mon, Ma. You're overreacting."

"No, I'm not. We raised y'all to be Christians. The religion America was founded on."

"Don't act like all Christians is good, Mom. It ain't no secret some of those Christian judges, politicians, and police officers are some of the worst criminals to walk the face of the Earth. They do dirt all week long, and then smile in church on Sunday. And I'm not sayin' all Muslims is good, either. Al-Qaeda and 9-11 attest to that. But Barron is your son, Mom."

"Hmph," she mumbled, rolling her eyes at me. At 52, my mother still held onto some of her youthful jubilance. She taught English at Rufus King High School, and the teenagers kept her hip to the latest fads and lingo.

"Have you spoken to your father?" she asked as I roamed the fridge for leftovers.

"Nah. But I will catch him before I leave. He here?" I asked as I pulled out a plate of liver smothered in gravy.

"He's in the basement. In his 'man cave,'" she joked.

Hearing her say 'man cave' made me laugh and almost drop the bowl of potatoes I had just grabbed. "Is that what he callin' it?"

"That's not what he is calling it. That's what I call it. I saw somebody say it on TV and it stuck."

The area of the house Mom was talking about used to be the rec room when I was growing up. Now that I had grown up and Barron was in prison, Pop turned the area into his own space. And even though he had been with Mom since she was sixteen, wasn't she or nobody else allowed into the 'man cave' without permission.

"I'ma check on him as soon as I finish fixing my plate."

"So, when are you going to find a woman you can settle down with, son? You're 27. I'm not going to be cooking for your butt much longer. Don't you think it's about time you stopped being a bachelor and brought one of them girls home to meet us?"

"C'mon, Mom. I don't wanna go there with you. I tried settling down. Remember? Didn't got that well. Worst mistake I ever made. I don't like making the same mistakes. And I ain't."

"'Ain't' is not a word. And what do you mean, you don't want to go there with me? I am your mother. You will go wherever I take you."

"Alright. I'll make you a deal. A one time offer. You stop trying to get in my love life, and I'll go to church with you on Sunday. Deal?"

I didn't like discussing my love life with my mom. I wasn't ready to settle down. I liked variety. And spice. But that wasn't in line with the Christian principles I was raised by. And since I didn't feel like being lectured on God's ideal for our relationships, I gave her a bone.

"You think you slick, don't you?" Mom asked, seeing

through my attempt to get her out of my business.

"So, is that a deal?" I asked, sticking to the script. Mom had been trying to get me to go to church with her for months, but I always had an excuse. It wasn't that I didn't like church, because I did. I just hated getting up on Sunday mornings. That was my day off. A day I normally filled with sleeping late and kinky sex.

"Your negotiating skills have gotten better, son. Good job," Mom smiled.

"Deal or no deal?" I pressed.

"Deal. If me staying out of your business will get you into the Lord's house, then don't ever tell me nothing else."

I could see the wheels turning in her mind as she smiled at me lovingly. I knew she would try to pair me with one of her friend's daughters or one of the church's 'good girls'. Little did she know, that's what I wanted her to do. Church girls were freaks. The last time I went to church with her, my bed springs got a ton of work.

After fixing my plate, I headed to the basement to check on Pop.

"What you got on that plate, boy?" Pop asked as I plopped down on the couch in the man cave. He was busy working on an old school floor model TV.

"Liver. Potatoes. Who decorates a man cave with a floor model TV?" I asked between bites.

"Put that plate down and help me real quick. I gotta get this picture tube in."

I reluctantly sat my plate on the table in front of the couch and went to help him. "Why don't you just buy a new TV, Pop? You just wasting money buying parts."

"'Cause this is a family heirloom. This is priceless."

"You right about this being priceless. Won't nobody put a price on this old joker," I cracked.

Pop didn't find my joke funny. My dad wasn't a joker. He was a serious man who felt joking was a waste of time. I wondered how Mom had dealt with his serious demeanor for over thirty years.

"See, that's what's wrong with your generation. Y'all all jacked up and broke because y'all play too much and y'all too materialistic. Don't appreciate the old school. Back in my–"

My phone rang, cutting him off. I was glad. Pop could go on some serious rants. "Hold on, Pops." I checked the screen on my phone and seen it was Latia. I couldn't wipe the smile off my face as I answered. "Hey, baby girl."

"Daddy, can you come and get me?" she cried.

I felt my pulse quicken as my parental instincts set in. "Latia, what's wrong?"

"Momma and Pistol fighting again."

I could feel my blood begin to boil. "Where they at now?"

"Downstairs. I'm up in my room."

"Okay. Stay in your room. I'm on my way."

"What's up?" Pop asked, staring at me intently as I hung up the phone.

"Shay and her boyfriend fighting again. Latia scared."

"You want me to come with you?" he offered. Pop was from the south. Mississippi. He didn't believe in hitting women. Felt the men who did were cowards. Cowards who needed tuning up. Hood-style.

"Nah, Pop. I got this. I'll call you later."

I ran up the stairs and out of the house like a man on a mission. I hopped in my black F-150 and sped toward Shay's house, all the while thinking about beating Shay and Pistol's asses. Shay was lucky Pop taught me not to hit women. Otherwise, I would have knocked her out years ago. Pistol, however, was another story.

When I pulled up to Shay's house, I mashed my brakes, bringing my truck to a screeching stop to let them know I was there. I hopped out of my truck and ran up on the porch. I tried the door. It was locked. I beat on it like I was the police.

"Who is it?" Shay called from the inside.

"Luke! Open this door!"

I heard locks click, and when the door cracked open, I barged in. "What the fuck is yo' problem, Shay? What I tell you 'bout fighting with yo' niggas around Latia?" I yelled, getting in her face.

"Get outta my house, Luke!" She pushed me. "Don't come in here tellin' me how to run my shit. And how you know what go on in my house, nigga?"

"Latia called me. What I tell you 'bout that shit? Fuck is y'all problem?"

"Fuck you, Luke. This my house. I do what the fuck I want wit' whoever I want. You don't pay no bills here, nigga."

"I know y'all better quit fighting around my daughter," I threatened, mean-mugging her.

Shay was a small woman. 5'5", 125 pounds with crazy curves. She had mocha skin, juicy lips, and wore her hair in a choppy do. She wasn't the finest woman I had ever been with, but what she lacked in beauty she made up with in sex appeal. And even though she was tiny compared to me, what she lacked in height and weight she made up with her heart and her slick mouth.

"Or what? Big Chief locked up. What chu gon' do, college boy?" she mocked.

"Yeah. What chu gon' do, nigga?" Pistol asked, appearing out of thin air.

Pistol was Shay's boyfriend of the last seven or eight months. He was a little man who stood about 5'6" and weighed about 150 pounds soaking wet. I was 6'3" and 220 pounds. A giant compared to him. But the thing about Pistol was he had earned his name. He always kept a gun and wouldn't hesitate to use it.

Pistol knew I wasn't in the streets and didn't own a gun, but he also knew who my big brother was. Everybody in Milwaukee knew Big Chief. Pistol also knew my bro wasn't around to fight my battles anymore, but I couldn't back down from him. Not in front of Shay. And not while my daughter was upstairs. I knew she was listening.

"Listen, man. I ain't trynna go there with you, but y'all ain't finna be fighting around my daughter."

"Nigga, this my shit. I'm the king of this castle. I do what the fuck I want. You or yo' daughter don't like it, you and that heffa can kick rocks."

"You betta watch yo' mouth, chump!" I threatened, clenching my fists and walking toward him.

Pistol pulled out a black automatic handgun.

"No, Luke," Shay grabbed me.

"Listen to yo' B.M., Luke. Fuck around and getcho shit split," Pistol mugged me.

"You a pussy-nigga. Only cowards hit women. Put that pistol down and I'll whoop yo' ass."

"Nigga, say one mo' word and I'ma blaze yo' bitch-ass!" he threatened, clicking the safety off his gun.

He had the upper hand. I was mad, but I was no fool, so I turned to Shay. "Go get my daughter. I'm taking her with me."

"No, Luke. Just leave. We'll talk later. Please." She begged, looking at me with pleading eyes.

I could tell she feared for my safety, but I wasn't leaving

without my daughter. "Hell, nah! I ain't leaving her here. Go get her. Latia! Latia! Come downstairs!" I called up the stairwell.

"Luke, stop! Get out!" Shay yelled. I ignored her.

"Latia! Latia."

"Daddy!" Latia called as she came running out of her room.

Latia was an average-sized seven-year-old. She had a light brown complexion, her hair done up in pigtails that came to her shoulders, and a personality as big as the sun. But her personality wasn't showing as she bounced down the stairs. I seen fear and uncertainty in her eyes.

"Latia, go back to your room!" Shay yelled.

"No. Come here, baby. You leaving with me," I countered.

Latia stopped in the middle of the stairwell, looking back and forth from me to her mother. She was confused. Didn't know which parent to listen to.

"Go back to yo' room," Pistol cut in.

Oh, hell nah! "Don't tell my daughter what to do, nigga!" I barked.

"Or what? Fuck you gon' do?" he challenged, clutching his pistol tighter as a snarl spread across his ugly face.

"Luke, you good, nigga?" a deep voice called from behind me. I knew the voice. And so did Pistol.

"Trigga! What up, bra?" I spun to greet my long-time friend. I was surprised he was there, but I was happy as hell to see him.

"Pop called and said you needed help. You good?" Trigga asked, mean-mugging Shay and Pistol.

When I looked back at Bonnie and Clyde, they both looked terrified. Pistol had even put his gun away.

"Yeah, Trigga. Everything good. I was just coming to get

Latia. Ain't that right, Pistol?" I asked, daring him to get bold in front of Trigga.

The look on Pistol's face was priceless. He looked like he was about to piss on himself. "Yeah. We good," he mumbled, refusing to look me and Trigga in our eyes.

Chapter 8

"You listenin' to me, Syn?" Seven asked, giving me a hard stare from the other side of the table.

"Yeah, I hear you. And the answer is no."

"But, Syn, this bitch will have niggas cashin' out. We–"

"No, Seven! Ain't no young girls dancing in my club! I don't care how grown she looks. She's sixteen. A minor. That's a case."

Seven's eyes turned into angry slits as he stared at me. He wasn't used to women getting loud with him. I could tell he wanted to put his hands on me, and he probably would've if he hadn't known my past.

"A'ight, Syn. That's yo' shit. I respect that," he sulked, pulling the toothpick from his mouth and sucking his teeth.

I liked Seven as a business partner. When I first started my club, some of the first girls I hired came from his flock. After my club started turning a profit and I was able to hire a full staff of my own girls, I parted ways with Seven. But we still did business every now and then.

"Good. Glad we got that understanding. Now–" I was saying when he put up a hand, stopping me mid-sentence.

"Hold on. I need to get this," he said as he reached for his phone. When I nodded, he got up and walked away.

While Seven and his tailored, blue-pinstriped Armani suit strolled away for privacy, I picked up my glass of Moscato and let my eyes dance around the watering hole. The place was called Joey's, a hip and expensive social gathering place in downtown Milwaukee. Joey's clientele consisted of Milwaukee's finest. Corporate men and women, business owners, athletes, and politicians. The dress code in Joey's was strict. No tennis shoes, t-shirts, and no wannabe ballers with shiny jewelry trying to make it rain. Just how I liked it. As the owner of a strip club, I had seen enough paper bills falling from the ceiling. It got old.

"May I?" a deep voice asked from my right.

I looked over and seen a dark-skinned giant smiling down at me. The man looked to be about 6'6", long-limbed, and skinny with shoulder-length dreadlocks. He was wearing a dark-colored, tailored suit. I'd seen him before. On TV. He was an NBA player. I couldn't remember his name, but I knew he played for the home team.

"Sorry, I'm kinda bu–"

"I noticed you from across the room, lookin' like somethin' fresh outta my dreams," he cut me off, licking his lips as he sat in Seven's seat.

On any other day I probably would've given him a shot, but today I was all business. After my meeting with Seven, I had to meet with a lingerie designer who wanted my girls to wear merchandise. And for that reason, Mr. NBA had to go.

"Um, sorry, but I don't–"

"I knew I had to come shoot my shot 'fore that metrosexual-lookin'-ass nigga came back. You need a real man, ma. Somebody who can take you on trips, shoppin', and show you the finer things in life. So, what up? Gimme yo' numba."

I was shocked. Not only was he rude, but he was also clueless. I had to put him in his place. Let him know I was not interested in him, nor did I need a man to take care of me. My crisp white Louie coat and Chloe trousers screamed money.

"Can you afford me?" I asked, challenging him with my stare.

He looked at me like I had spit on him. "Baby girl, I can buy you a new life."

"Well, baby boy, my kitty don't purr for nothing less

than seven figures. Wanna play?"

"Seven figures?" he scoffed.

"Gotta pay to play," I smiled.

"You on some bullshit, ma. Ain't nobody givin' a mill to fuck."

I crossed my arms and sat back in my chair. "Well then, we done talking."

"Stuck-up-ass bitch!" he cursed as he got up from the table.

I was laughing on the inside, but I kept a stone look on my face. "You probably got a li'l dick anyway," I called after him.

The hoopster stopped and spun to face me. I had hit his sore spot. Uh-oh!

"Bitch, I–" he was saying, but stopped. His eyes focused on something to my left. I looked and seen Seven walking in our direction. I smiled at the baller's cowardice. He gave me an angry leer before walking away.

"Ay, Syn. Shit gettin' hectic on my end. I gotta run. Alphabet boys on my ass," Seven yelled as he strolled past me, never breaking his stride. His eyes were wide and he looked scared. Like jail was imminent.

"Okay, babe. Call me later," I called after him. He didn't respond.

When Seven left the club, I reached in my Prada bag to get my phone. I needed to check the time. It was 10:49 P.M. I had about ten minutes to kill until my next meeting. I was tucking my phone back into my purse when I looked up and seen the dreadlocked baller heading in my direction. He had a hard stare on his face and was walking with a purpose.

Shit! I reached into my bag and clutched the butt of my .380 Smith & Wesson.

"Yeah, bitch! Talk that–"

"Yo, Maurice!" a brown-skinned man wearing a lavender suit called as he walked up behind the ball player.

Mr. NBA gave a strained look as he spun to see who had called him. He and the new guy locked eyes for a moment before recognition set in. "Cool-Hand Luke! What up, nigga?" the baller beamed as he and the man in the lavender suit hugged like they were long-lost brothers.

I kept my hand on my gun as I watched them.

"Yo! What up, Big Mo? Seen you drop thirty-five on Miami last night."

"Aw, man. You know they can't hold me. They should call me flash," he laughed, seeming to forget about me.

"Hey, man. Come get a drink with yo' boy. It's been awhile," Cool-Hand Luke said, wrapping an arm around Big Mo's shoulder. They turned and began walking toward the bar when Cool-Hand Luke looked back at me. We had a brief staring contest before his eyes traveled down to my hand in my purse. When his eyes met mine again, he gave me a knowing smile before walking away with his friend.

"Whew!" I breathed a sigh of relief. I didn't want to have to shoot Milwaukee's playoff hope, but I would've. Thank God for good samaritans.

I took a sip of my drink and waited a few more minutes for my next meeting. The time ticked by slowly, and when I checked the time again, I seen it was ten minutes past 11 o'clock. After sending the lingerie designer a nasty text for standing me up, I prepared to leave.

"Sorry about my friend," lavender suit said, appearing out of nowhere. He was hovering over the seat Seven and Big Mo had shared.

"It's okay. Is that why you came over? To apologize?" I asked, checking him out.

He was handsome in a distinguished sort of way. And

well-groomed. He wore lavender alligator shoes with his nicely-cut lavender suit. I could tell he was a professional man. Maybe a lawyer.

"Are you always this straightforward?" he asked, giving a light chuckle. His eyes were piercing. I could tell he was a womanizer. A smooth operator.

"I don't bullshit because I don't like bullshit," I said, holding his stare.

"Well, good. Bullshitting is a character flaw, and my genes are great. May I sit down?"

I liked him. His aura. He was confidant. But I wasn't easy. "Why?"

"Because you want me to. Otherwise you would have insulted my manhood. Like you did Maurice," he smiled. It was a good smile. Nice teeth.

"Sure. Have a seat, Mr....?"

"Luke. Luke Swanson." He extended his hand as he sat. I shook.

"Okay, Luke. But I'm not telling you my last name."

"That's okay. I like mystery," he flirted, giving me another sexy smile. A smile I was growing to like.

"So, to what do I owe the pleasure, Luke?"

"Well, miss, I have good news and bad news. The bad news is I didn't come over just to apologize for my college teammate. The good news is, I don't plan on leaving without your number."

I liked him. Problem was, he was starting to get cocky. He knew I liked him and was going to give him my number. So I didn't. "Sorry, Luke. It takes more than an apology, an expensive suit, and a nice smile to get my number," I said, grabbing my purse as I stood to my feet.

He continued to sit, watching me, a confident smile etched on his face. "Do you know what destiny is?" he asked.

"Yeah. It's what's meant to happen."

"Funny thing about destiny is, it's not about what happens to you, but how you react to what happens to you."

I liked that, but I didn't let him know it.

"Bye, Luke."

Chapter 9

Church girls are straight-up freaks! If the Lord was looking down on us right now, I hoped the blood those preachers said covered our sins had gotten in God's eyes, blurring his vision.

"Oh, God! Oh, God! Oh, God!" Shayna moaned, crying out the savior's name as she ground her twat on my face. She had one of the best looking pussies I had ever seen. Brazilian waxed. No hair bumps. As fat as a camel's toe. And it tasted great! "Suck it, baby!" she moaned as I palmed her ass.

Shayna's body was crazy. Thick in all the right places. Booty big enough to set my beer on. Double-Ds up top. Flat stomach. Small waist. Skin the color of brown sugar. And she topped it all off with her baby face. Literally. She had just turned eighteen last week. Lucky me!

"Aw, shit, Luke! Mm. You got some good dick," Catrise moaned as she rode me like she had been doing rodeo all her life. Catrise was light-skinned, skinny, had full C-cup breasts, and freckles that covered most of her body. I met her when I went to church with mom two weeks ago. Her and Shayna were friends. I hadn't known Shayna that long. Maybe an hour. But I was definitely going to be seeing her again.

"Oh, my God! Oh, my God!" Shayna screamed as she shook and came all over my face. After getting her rocks off, she climbed off me and fell onto the bed. She began watching me and Catrise.

My second nut was taking a while, and if I could, I was going to hold out a little longer. I still needed to get inside of Shayna. "Take that dick, girl. Take it!" I encouraged Catrise as I placed my hands behind my head and watched her little booty jiggle. She was on me reverse cowgirl, working her hips like she was in a hula-hooping contest.

I felt the bed move. When I looked over, Shayna was crawling toward Catrise. I watched as she crawled in front of her and lowered her head.

"Oh, yes, girl. Oh, yes!" Catrise moaned.

I craned my neck to see what was going on. To my surprise, Shayna was sucking Catrise's pearl tongue as she rode me.

Straight-up freaks!

It didn't take Catrise long to cum. When she climbed off Givenchy, I locked eyes with Shayna.

"You ready for this shit?"

"Nah. You ready for this?" she sassed, rubbing her bald love spot.

On the strength she had a big booty, I had to hit it from the back. She climbed onto all fours in the middle of the bed, face down, ass up.

"Oh, Luke!" she cried, shooting her head up toward the ceiling as I slid deep into her.

Her insides felt like silk.

"Wait! Wait!"

"I knew you couldn't handle this dick," I bragged.

"Just wait. Hold on."

"Hell, nah. Fuck her, Luke. Fuck her!" Catrise cheered me on.

And I did.

***

I woke up the next morning to the sound of my phone vibrating on the hotel's bedside table. It was my alarm. I had set it for 6:00 A.M. Time for work.

"What time is it?" Catrise asked as I turned off the alarm.

"Six. I gotta go to work. Check out time is at noon," I told her as I climbed out of bed. My movement woke up Shayna.

"Luke, you wrong," Shayna whined.

"What are you talking about?" I asked as I slid into my jeans.

"My stuff sore. I think you broke something."

I couldn't help but laugh. "No pain, no gain!"

***

I left the girls at the Hyatt and dashed home to take a shower and dress. I lived in a two bedroom apartment on 29th and State. It was a mixed working class neighborhood. I had been meaning to get a house, but I hadn't gotten around to it yet. Plus, I liked my apartment. Lots of memories.

After letting myself in the lobby, I climbed the stairs to my second floor apartment. I left a trial of clothes from the front door to the bathroom as I went to shower. Twenty minutes later, I headed to the bedroom I had converted into a closet. I loved clothes, went shopping almost every weekend, and since I didn't have closets big enough to house all of my clothes, shoes, and jackets, I turned what used to be my guest bedroom into a closet. I had racks of clothes and shelves of shoes spread throughout the room like a clothing store.

I searched through the racks before settling on a suit from the Steve Harvey line. A plain black suit with a gray tie. After lotioning up and getting dressed, I sprayed on some Tom Ford cologne and I was out. I pulled into the parking lot of Marty and Sloan at 7:50. I had to be in by 8:00. Perfect timing.

Marty and Sloan was one of Milwaukee's most prestigious accounting firms. The firm only employed about twenty accountants and CPAs, but the clientele base was worth almost 200 million dollars. To work at Marty and Sloan, you had to know somebody who knew somebody. Most people who worked there got hired by word of mouth. Somebody had to literally vouch for them and accept responsibility for them before they would hire them.

What got me in was the word of my microeconomics professor in college. His brother worked for the firm. Because of my 4.5 GPA and my understanding of crunching numbers, he gave me the nod. I wouldn't have otherwise known about the firm, let alone got a job there.

"Good morning, Mr. Swanson," Ashley, one of our firm's receptionists, greeted me when I walked in. Ashley was a big-busted, green-eyed, moderately attractive, blonde-haired white woman in her mid-twenties. We had messed around a couple of times. What I liked about her was she loved to please. Loved it!

"Hey, Ashley. Looking good," I flirted as I breezed past her.

I was walking down the hall, headed for my office, when the door of the office next to mine opened up.

"Cool-Hand Luke! What's up, brother?" Travis smiled as he extended his hand.

Travis Kratz was my friend and mentor. We were both certified personal accountants at the firm. We did everything from taxes to investments. When I got hired at the company, Travis took me under his wing and showed me the ropes. Since we were the only two black men working in the firm, he made sure to go the extra mile to help me out.

"Travis, what's good, man?" I asked as we shook hands.

"The sun is shining, the birds are chirping, and I'm moving to New York." Travis had gotten a Job at Goldman Sachs. This was his final week on the job. I hated to see my friend go, but Goldman was more exclusive than Marty and Sloan. A once-in-a-lifetime opportunity.

"That's great, man. And if you ever wanna send me some tickets to a Knicks game, or even a Giants game, I'll still be here."

"Man, you know it don't matter where I go, I'll always be a fan of my Wisconsin teams. But I will be checking out the local NY teams. Melo!" he laughed, pretending to shoot a jump shot.

"Hey, we still on for that account you were telling me about last week?" I reminded him, like he had asked me to. For him to work with money, he had a terrible memory. I wondered how he got this far in the business with his memory problems.

"Oh, yeah, man. As a matter of fact, she will be coming to the office about ten. I assured her she would be in good hands."

When Travis found out he was going to Goldman, he had to transfer all his accounts throughout the firm. Marty and Sloan policy was we had to leave all our accounts when we left or were terminated.

"Okay. Say no more. I'll be in your office at 9:58," I assured him.

After unlocking the door to my office, I went inside and got comfy. I opened the blinds and powered on my computer before sitting at my desk to catch up on some work. I fumbled my way through spread sheets, losing track of time. I didn't know it was ten o'clock until Travis called me.

"Sorry I'm late," I apologized as I entered his office. Travis looked up from his desk and the client spun to face me. She was sitting in the chair in front of his desk. When we locked eyes, I smiled.

"Luke, this is Syncere Evans. Syncere, this is your new

money man, Luke Swanson," Travis introduced us.

"Should I be offended you are late for our first meeting?" Syncere asked.

"You should be impressed. The reason I'm late is because I was working. I am dedicated to my job and clients. This is a sign I will put everything on hold to take care of something I'm responsible for."

"Or maybe it means you can't handle your business as well as you think you can," she said, looking me up and down.

I could've sworn her eyes rested on my crotch for a split second. "If you want, I will give you the numbers of all twelve of my clients. I'm sure they will tell you how well I *satisfy* them," I said, putting emphasis on 'satisfy.' She had delivered an innuendo, and I gave it right back.

"Wait. Have you two met?" Travis asked, looking back and forth between me and Syncere.

"We had a run-in about a week ago," I answered, my eyes never leaving hers.

"Well, Miss Evans, I assure you that you are in good hands. Luke is one of our firm's best and brightest. I trained him myself," Travis bragged, sounding like a proud father.

"I do hope you are right, Travis," Syncere said, still holding my stare.

"He is," I cut in.

"Luke, I was just telling Miss Evans about a new real estate project going on in Illinois. I was thinking–"

"Excuse me, Travis," I cut him off, turning to Syncere. "Would you mind finishing this meeting in my office?"

I loved my boy Travis like he was a brother, but I wasn't about to let him make me look like a Boy Scout in front of Syncere. I needed to introduce her to my plans. Show her I was on top of my game. Plus, she was sending me vibes I wanted to get her alone to explore.

"Uh, sure," she accepted, looking surprised by my move.

"Excuse us, Travis," I said, extending my hand to help Syncere out of her seat.

Travis looked up at me with questioning eyes. I mouthed, *"Sorry, bro,"* to him as I escorted Syncere toward the door.

"My office is next door," I said as I opened the door. When Syncere walked out into the hall in front of me, I took the time to check out her body. It was a work of art. The blue skinny jeans she wore accentuated her hips, thighs, and butt. And the red bottoms she wore made her ass sit high in the sky like it was the sun.

"So, Mr. Smooth is an accountant, huh?" she asked as we walked into my office.

"And a damned good one, too. Have a seat. Would you like something to drink?"

"Travis never offered me a beverage. I'm starting to think he may have been right about you. I'll have a water," she said as she sat down in the chair across from my desk.

"A'ight," I nodded, buzzing one of the secretaries.

"Yes, Mr. Swanson," Ashley answered.

"Can you bring me two waters? I would be forever indebted."

"No problem," she giggled.

"She a fan?" Syncere asked after I clicked off the intercom.

"I'm not famous. I don't have groupies. Now, where were we?" I asked, wanting to focus on business.

"You were about to tell me your plans to help make my money grow," she said, licking her lips seductively.

I gave a smirk as I opened up the file I had gotten from Travis. "I see Travis has you spread out," I paused, looking up to see if she had caught my innuendo. She had. "In a few different bonds, IRAs, and stocks. The bull is at a record pace right now, so any long-term investments will continue to grow. Some of these I would advise you to trade or sell. For example, the Facebook IPO, J.C. Penny, and K-Mart. J.C. Penny and K-Mart finished the last quarter in the red. You only have a couple shares of each one, so they shouldn't be hard to dump."

"And where should I re-invest?" she asked as the door to my office opened. Ashley came in and gave me two bottles of water before sashaying from the room. I gave one of the bottles to Syncere and opened my own.

"I knew what Travis was trying to do by buying shares from these places. They were cheap, low-risk, and he was looking for these companies to bounce back next quarter. But they are not going to bounce back. I suggest getting some shares of Yahoo and getting a head start in buying up shares of this new battery company called A-Batteries."

She took a small diva sip from her bottle of water before responding. "You sound like you know what you're talking about."

"I do."

"Cocky?" she questioned, raising an eyebrow.

"Confidant."

"Spoiled," she teased.

"A go-getter."

Her smile vanished as we began a staring contest. Her eye contact was strong. Un-blinking. I could tell she was a strong woman. If she had a man, or woman, I knew she wore the pants in the relationship. Her eyes spoke of a strength and experience that was battle-tested. A strength and experience I wanted to know more about.

"Can I trust you?" she asked, breaking the silence, but not the stare.

"With your life."

"I trust no one with my life. I'm talking about my money."

"That, too."

Her smile returned. Only it wasn't an amused smile. It was an 'I like you' smile. "Good," she said, placing her hands on the armrests, about to stand and leave.

"Do you remember what I said about destiny?" I asked, keeping her seated.

She eyed me as she thought for a few moments. "Something about us being able to choose it."

I knew she misquoted me on purpose. It was her attempt to act aloof and uncaring. Like my words didn't matter. "Actually, I said, 'It's not what happens to you, but how you react to what happens to you.' This is destiny. So, when can I take you out?"

"You don't want to take me out. Your ego can't handle me."

"I don't have an ego. Egos are for men with small packages who are sensitive and bruise easily. I don't bruise. Nor is my package small."

"Superman, huh?"

"Nah. A go-getter. I already told you that. I get what I want."

"I don't mix business with pleasure," she said, finally standing.

"You will."

Another stare down ensued. This one didn't last as long as the first because she looked away. I had bested her in the staring contest.

"Have a good day, Mr. Swanson," she said, smoothing the wrinkles that had formed on the thighs of her pants as she walked toward the door.

I remained seated as I watched her pretty, brown, round behind bounce and sway as she walked. "I will keep you posted on my progress."

"Do that," she called over her shoulder.

"Fate has given me your number. I'll be in touch."

She paused at the door, spinning to face me. She looked like she wanted to say something. I waited. Apparently at a loss for words, she gave me a smile and wink before letting herself out.

Chapter 10

"Who was that?" Stephen asked angrily after I hung up the phone.

"Excuse me?" I asked, looking at him like he had called me a dirty name.

Stephen shifted nervously in his seat. "My bad. Should I call the waiter? Ready to go?"

I suppressed my grin. "No. I'll do that," I said, signaling the waiter who was heading in our direction.

Stephen busied himself with an invisible spot on his green polo shirt while I paid for our meals. As I looked over at him, I couldn't help but think how he disgusted me. He was weak and had no brains, drive, guts, or backbone. I had been seeing him for almost six months, exclusively on my terms. He was my twenty-five-year-old boy-toy. Whenever I had an itch, he scratched it. When I told him to jump, he asked, "How high?"

The crazy thing about him was Stephen looked like a manly-man. He looked like he would fit right in on any corner in any of the inner cities. He stood 6'1", had a muscular build, walked with swagger, and had a big dick. Not to mention his excellent sex skills. But he was weak and let me walk all over him. If it wasn't for his skills in the bedroom, I would've kicked him to the curb. But good dick was hard to find, so I kept him around.

"I'll be back. I have to go powder my nose," I said, standing to my feet and grabbing my Gucci tote.

Stephen stood with me, being the perfect gentleman. I liked a man with manners, but his act of chivalry made him seem even softer. I knew I wouldn't be seeing him for a few weeks.

After using the bathroom, I walked over to the giant

vanity mirror above the sink and stared at my reflection as I washed my hands. I looked into my hazel-brown eyes and thought about the meeting I had with Luke Swanson a few hours ago. He was interesting. And he had bested me in the staring contest. I didn't like that. My stare usually intimidated people, men and women alike. Most people cowered under a long, hard stare. But not Luke. I knew there was something different about him when I met him at Joey's. I knew I had done the right thing by not giving him my number. Problem was, he had gotten it anyway, and then some. It made me wonder if he knew something about destiny I didn't.

"Let's go," I called out to Stephen as I walked back to our table.

He leapt out the chair with the swiftness of a cheetah. "Here's your credit card. Should I get the car?"

"Yes. Do that. I have to make a call," I told him as I pocketed my platinum card and handed him the keys to my sports car.

While he went to go fetch my car, I stood under the restaurant's awning and waited. I didn't have a phone call to make. I just wanted to make him work.

***

"You want to come in?" Stephen asked, interrupting my thoughts.

I looked around and seen we were outside his small, four-apartment tenement on the west side of Milwaukee.

"Um, what?" I asked, snapping out of my fog. I didn't hear what he said because I was busy thinking of a way to get my club more exposure.

"Is everything okay?" he asked, looking at me

suspiciously.

"Yeah. I'm fine. Get out. I have to go," I said, motioning for him to get out of the car.

When he got out, I slid into the driver's seat. I noticed he was still standing next to my car. I gave him the 'what do you want?' look.

"You sure you don't want to come in?"

When I seen the lustful look in his eyes, I got turned on. "On second thought, yeah."

As soon as we got into his living room, we got right to it. No kissing or touching. He wasn't my man, and I didn't want foreplay. I wanted one thing: an orgasm. So, after we got naked, I told him to lay on the couch and I sat on his face. I rode his lips until I was ready to cum

"Stick your tongue in me," I told him, taking my clit from his mouth. Stephen had a long tongue, and I loved riding it when I came.

"Oh, yeah!" I moaned when his warm tongue slipped inside of me. I didn't waste time getting my rocks off. I pressed all of my weight on his face, trying to get as much of his tongue inside of me as I could. Then I rode him until he was drowning in my juices. My orgasm was epic! His face glistened from my nectar as I slid down onto his chiseled chest. He looked up at me with horny eyes. I knew the look. He wanted his.

"Where are your rubbers?" I asked.

"In my pants pocket."

I stood, grabbed his pants from the floor, and searched his pockets. When I found the Magnum, I looked down at his throbbing meat. It looked like a silo. Like he was ready to do some damage. But not today. Today, I was in control.

After I slid the condom on him, I mounted him reverse cowgirl. I didn't want to see his face.

"Oh, yeah, Syn. You feel so good," he moaned as I sat down on him. I let out a few moans of my own.

I liked riding Stephen. He was the perfect size and length. Long enough to go deep without punching a hole in me, and thick enough to fill me up. It didn't take long for both of us to get our fix, and my second orgasm drained me, putting me to sleep.

***

"Shh. Just come back later."

My eyes shot open. I looked around and seen I was lying in Stephen's bed, a sheet on top of me. And Stephen was gone.

"No, Stephen! Let me in right now!" a woman screamed.

I shot out of bed, wrapping a sheet around me as I ran to the bedroom door. I peeked out and seen Stephen standing at the front door in his boxers. The door was partially opened, the chain keeping it from opening all the way. I couldn't see who he was talking to because his body was blocking my view.

"Carmen, just come back later. I told you to call before you come over. You can't just be showing up," Stephen whispered.

"Do you have another bitch in there? Open this damn door right now, Stephen!"

"Yo, Carmen, chill! You gon' start my neighbors to trippin'! Ain't nobody in here. Come back later."

"Fuck that! Let me in!" the woman screamed.

Stephen stepped back as an arm flew through the door. "Aye, you trippin'! Move!" Stephen yelled as he forced her arm out of the door and shut it.

"She sounds crazy," I muttered as I walked out of the

bedroom.

"S-sorry 'bout that. I told her to call first. I'm trynna make her leave."

"Stephen, open this door! I hear you in there. Who you talking to?" Carmen yelled as she beat on the door.

"That's your girl, huh?" I asked as I began putting on my clothes.

"Something like that. But you know you–"

"Save that shit," I cut him off. "I don't care who you fuck. Just keep yo' hos in check."

"Open this door, Stephen!" Carmen continued to shout.

"This bitch is crazy! Damn, I wish I never woulda fucked her."

"That's what happens when you think with your dick," I laughed as I slid into my blouse.

"Syn, can you do me a favor and leave out the window?" Stephen asked.

I looked up from putting on my heels to see if he was serious. He was. And he was wearing a sad puppy dog look on his face. The look was meant to draw sympathy, but all it did was made me realize how pathetic he was.

"Hell nah, nigga! You out cho rabbit-ass mind?" I couldn't believe he had asked me that. "I don't do closets or windows, Stephen. I'm a Boss Bitch. I'm walkin' out the same door I came in. Yo' bitch betta recognize!"

"Syn, please. I–"

"Stephen, open this fucking door!" Carmen's shriek cut him off.

"Open the door, Stephen," I said firmly. I was leaving, and I dared this bitch to test me.

"Syn, this shit–"

"Open the door!" I demanded.

He stared at me to see if I would change my stance. I

didn't. I was ready to go.

"A'ight," he sighed as he moped over and began unlocking the door.

"Motherfucker, I told you–" Carmen yelled as she burst into the apartment. When she seen me standing in the middle of the living room, she stopped. A stare down ensued.

Carmen was average-looking. A little chubby with big lips, big breasts, and a stupid booty. She was looking at me like she wanted to try me, assessing whether or not she thought she could take me.

"Oh, hell nah, Stephen! Who the fuck is this bitch?" she asked, never taking her eye off me.

"Yo, Carmen, chill. This my cousin. She 'bout to leave," Stephen lied.

She pushed him hard and sent him crashing into the wall. She looked back at me with a fire in her eyes, and then she rushed me.

"Unless you want to die, you better move yo' ass out of my way!" I threatened, pointing my .380 at her. I knew she was about to try something, and I already had my hand inside my bag.

She stopped in her tracks. I could see the anger and fear swirling around in her eyes.

"You can keep your man. I don't want him. But we ain't about to fight over no dick. Too many out there to be fighting over one." After I said my piece, I eased by her and headed toward the door. "Lose my number, Stephen. I don't got time for this shit," I called as I left the apartment.

I was busy tucking my gun in my purse when I collided with a woman who was entering the building.

"Oh! Excuse me," I apologized.

"Oh, I'm sorry. I didn't see you," she apologized, looking up from her phone.

When we locked eyes, I recognized her immediately. It had been almost two decades since I'd last seen her, and she had put on some pounds, but it was her. I was sure. Dark skin, big breasts, and the apple shape.

"It's okay. I'm alright," I said quickly, making a bee-line from the building before she recognized me.

"Loretta!" she called.

I didn't turn around. I trotted to my car and sped away.

J-Blunt

Chapter 11

"Cool-Hand Luke!" Trigga called as we shook hands and exchanged half-hugs.

"What's good, Trigga man?" I smiled.

"Shit, was wonderin' if yo' ass was gon' make it. We got mad bitches, blunts, and bub, my nigga. This a celebration." He smiled as he led me into a house I had never been to.

Trigga was my best friend. Growing up, we were like brothers. We had known each other since grade school. He stood a little over six feet and had a muscular build from constantly being in and out of jail. His skin was Hershey dark, and he wore his hair in cornrows that came just past his shoulders.

"I see y'all gettin' it in," I commented as he led me through the house that looked like a mix between a castle and a frat house. The music boomed from speakers placed throughout the house, making it sound as if we were at a concert, and everybody we walked past was smoking or drinking something mind-altering.

"Hit up the bar wit' me, nigga," Trigga said as he led me into the basement. The lower level of the house looked more like a club than a basement. A fully-stocked bar, pool tables, couches, chairs, and tables were spread throughout the basement. It even had a movie showing on a projection screen. *Paid In Full*, I think. But what caught my eye was the strippers. Five of them.

"Now, this is a party!" I laughed, watching a big-busted, dark-skinned woman giving one of Trigga's guys the lap dance of the century.

"You know how I do it. Go hard or go home," he told me before turning to the bar keeper. "Ariel, gimme two bottle of Ciroc."

"How much a party like this cost?" I asked. If possible, I wanted to repeat this atmosphere for my next birthday bash.

"Can't put a price on fun, Luke. And you not wearing that Brooks Brothers-ass suit to questions, nigga," he said, giving my beige K&G suit the once-over.

"I just got off work, man. Beside, ladies love a man in a suit. That's my swag," I laughed, grabbing the bottle of Ciroc the dreadlocked bartender sat on the bar.

"Well, I hate to tell you, partner, but ain't no ladies gon' be around tonight. Only hos. And hos don't give a fuck about a nigga in a suit. Ain't Big Chief taught you better than that?"

"Ha! Funny!" I laughed as I took a sip of my drink.

"So, how my nigga doin', anyway? Heard you went to see him a li'l while ago."

"Bro is good, Trigga. Holding his head up and still fighting for his freedom. Told me to tell you what's up and to get at him."

"I'ma do that. Fucked up how they did my nigga. He was the realest nigga I ever met. Saved my fuckin' life. If it wasn't for Chief, ain't no tellin' where I would be."

"Yeah. He responsible for turning Corey into Trigga man!" I laughed.

"Don't be sayin' my government name out loud, nigga!" Trigga scolded. "But shit, er'body wasn't destined for that college shit like you. Some of us had to hit the streets for a meal. Niggas' ribs get to touchin', that school shit is the first thing to go."

"Yeah, I feel you. But you ever wish you could do it all over? Do something different?" I asked, taking another sip of my drink.

Trigga took a long sip from his bottle before answering. "Hell yeah! Every nigga that been through what I have would say the same thang. Killin' niggas is gettin' old. Gotta watch my back from the niggas that want to take my spot. Gotta watch the police. Can't trust these bitches. And I always gotta be on my toes 'cause the same muthafuckas thata pay me to whack a nigga will fuck around and turn me in if they get caught. But you? You get paid to use yo' brain to make money. Gettin' muthafuckas rich the legit way. Don't gotta worry 'bout duckin' strays. Shit, sometimes I envy you, nigga. Big Chief saved you from this shit."

I had no comment. Trigga had spoken the truth. While my parents raised me right and made sacrifices so I could attend the University of Illinois, Big Chief did everything in his power to keep me away from the streets. Trigga didn't have the same support system. By the time we made it to high school, he was barely coming to class. And when I left for college, he became my brother's enforcer and bodyguard. He had a lot of blood on his hands. Killing was all he knew.

"Where you get the girls from?" I asked, looking around at the handful of half-naked women strutting around.

"Fam, you heard about that strip club, The Den of Syn?"

I smiled as I thought about Syncere. "Yeah, I heard of it. Never been, though."

"We gon' have to change that. Got some of the baddest hos in the Midwest up in there. That's where these bitches from."

"Oh, yeah? Man, I just met the owner about a week ago."

"Word? Man, you ain't–"

Trigga stopped. Something across the room caught his eye. "Hold on, fam. Aye, Silk! What I tell you 'bout that shit, nigga?" Trigga yelled as he leapt up from the bar stool.

I looked in the direction he was heading and seen the big-busted lap dancer in a wrestling match with the man she had been giving the lap dance to. I couldn't hear their words over the music, but I knew they were yelling at each other.

"Hey, handsome," a woman's voice said, pulling my attention away from the confrontation. I looked to my right and seen one of the exotic dancers standing next to me. She looked like a mix between Raven Symone and Nikki Minaj. Light-skinned, long hair, and thicker than a Snickers. She was wearing black boy shorts covered in rhinestones, a black bra also covered in rhinestones, and black four-inch pumps.

"Hey, young lady," I said, ignoring Trigga as he roughly escorted Silk up the stairs.

"I was hoping I could give you some company," she said, flashing a smile as she placed a hand on my thigh.

"Please do. My boy just left, and I need some company."

"The mani and suit is smooth, too. What would you like me to do?" she asked as she spread my legs and walked in-between.

"Surprise me."

"How do you like this?" she asked, turning around and sitting one of the softest asses I ever felt on my lap.

Givenchy jumped to attention. "If this is wrong, I don't want to be right."

"So, what is your name, suit man?"

"Luke. I'm actually a friend of your boss."

"Really? You know Syncere?" she asked. I could hear the excitement in her voice.

"Something like that."

"Well, you make sure you tell her how good Ferrary treated you. And if you ever in the club, make sure to holla."

"I'll do you one better. I'ma call her now," I said, fishing my phone from the breast pocket of my jacket. Ferrary continued to work on me as I dialed Syncere's number.

"Hey, money man. You're calling because you have good news, right?" she answered.

"Yeah. Something like that. I'm currently looking at your assets," I said, looking down at Ferrary's plump booty.

"Well, hopefully you're calling me to tell me you're making them grow."

"Something has grown, but not your assets."

"Luke, what the hell are you talking about? Why are you playing games?"

"I'm talking about the curves on your Ferrary. Beautiful ride. Handles nice."

Ferrary smiled back at me.

"Oh. I see," Syncere said, finally catching my drift. "Glad you like the service. Where are you?"

"At my boy's party. He hired your fleet."

"And where is Ferrary?"

"In the cockpit."

"Put her on."

I handed Ferrary the phone.

"Hey, boss lady. Okay. Mm-hm," she nodded, spinning to face me. "Okay. Got it," she smiled as she handed me back my phone. "This is from the boss," she said before kissing me on my neck a few times and massaging my pole through my pants.

Her tender, loving care felt great. Unfortunately, it was over just at quickly as it started.

"The dance was on the house," Ferrary said before strutting away.

"Was that a preview for the main event?" I asked Syncere as I watched Ferrary's ass jiggle away.

"There is no main event, Luke. That was me showing appreciation for you joining my team."

"Well, that means you still owe me."

"How do you figure?"

"Because those weren't your lips or hands."

"I have part ownership of everyone I employ."

"Not me," I clarified.

"Because I choose not to have it."

"Quite the contrary, Syncere. Whoever controls the purse, controls the strings. I have your purse," I smiled, liking the verbal tug-of-war.

"You are expendable," she countered.

Her comment was meant as a threat and a play to show her as my boss. She was pulling rank. I figured she expected me to bow down like most people. But I wasn't most people. I was Luke Swanson.

"So, expend me," I challenged.

"Is that a challenge?"

"It is whatever you want it to be."

Her end of the phone became silent. "What do you want, Luke?" I could hear the irritation in her voice.

"Dinner would be cool." She had already turned me down twice. I figured the third time might be the charm.

"I told you, I don't mix business with pleasure."

"Well, then, we will make this a business dinner."

"No, Luke."

"I thought you wanted to thank me?"

"I did."

"No, Ferrary did. You still owe me."

"Luke, I told you, I don't mix business–"

"I quit."

"What?" She asked. I could hear a little alarm in her voice.

"Since you don't want to mix business with pleasure, I quit," I clarified.

She laughed. "Luke, you're tripping."

"Dinner, Syncere. Or I walk," I threatened.

"No, you won't."

"You're not my only six-figure client. I think Bill Maggate has a thing for black women. I'ma e-mail him as soon as we're done."

"Luke, you are a pain in my ass," she sighed.

"Pain is pleasure," I laughed.

"Okay. We can do dinner. I will call you and let you know when and where."

I knew her setting the place and date was her attempt to hold onto some power. I let her have that. "Cool."

"Bye, Luke."

"Later," I said smoothly, smiling as I hung up the phone.

"These niggas be actin' like straight-up perverts!" Trigga vented as he sat down on the bar stool next to me.

I smiled over at him. Thoughts of Syncere had me feeling good.

"Fuck you smilin' like that for, nigga?"

J-Blunt

Chapter 12

"There was a time when our community was about oneness. Togetherness. Literally our brothers' and sisters' keepers. We knew on our own we were nothing, but we had strength in numbers," Luke said before taking a bite of his fillet mignon.

I liked him. Not only was he good looking, but he was smart. His knowledge about everything was vast. I enjoyed talking to him. So far we had talked about business, politics, and now we were in an in-depth discussion about black culture and black unity, or the lack thereof.

"Crack and the white folks," I added my two cents. "Regan-nomics did more damage to us than a lot of people realize. And now, with mass incarceration, unemployment and the fatherlessness epidemic, things seem to be worse."

"Yeah. In my opinion, fatherlessness is the biggest hindrance to us as a community. My father is the reason for my success. No doubt about that. He refused to let me be like my brother. Kept me busy with sports, boxing, and other activities."

"You don't look like a fighter," I smiled, looking him over. He wasn't a big man, maybe six feet and 200 pounds. The dark tailored suit did a good job of concealing what was underneath.

"What?" he asked, dropping his fork and putting up his dukes. "Golden Gloves city champ in Q7. Runner up in GR. I can hold my own."

"I bet I can take you," I challenged him. I wasn't flirting with him. I was testing him. Feeling him out. Seeing what I could get away with. Being around him made me feel inferior, like my feminine powers didn't work on him. I didn't like that.

"Only if I let you. And I would," he flirted, licking his lips.

He had full lips. And they were wet from his saliva and the meat. Looking at his lips turned me on. I wanted to kiss them and feel them on my nipples and clit. But I had to control myself. I wanted to be in charge.

"Tell me about your family," I said, switching subjects as I reached for my glass of Chardonnay.

"Mom and Pop been married for almost thirty years. She's a teacher and he's a laborer. Always worked with his hands. Preached to us about being a working man. 'If a man don't work, he don't eat,' he always said. We grew up in church. Every Sunday. But by the time I became a teenager, my brother stopped going. Began rebelling. Moved out when he was sixteen. My parents did everything possible to make sure I didn't follow in his steps."

"So, how is your brother doing now?" I asked. I could hear certain changes in his voice when he talked about his brother. Almost as if he had died.

"In prison. RICO Act," he said somberly.

"Sorry. Damn." I was at a loss for words. I wasn't expecting to hear that.

"Nah, it's cool. Bro lived fast. That kinda shit happens when you drive in that fast lane. So, tell me about you. Family and upbringing."

"Well, um, my life is complicated," I stuttered. I didn't dig into my past for nobody. Never got close enough to anybody to want to tell them. Had a hard time trusting people.

"Who's life isn't? My life ain't no crystal stair, either. Besides, you know all about me, and I don't know anything about you except your name, number, and that you own a strip club. I feel cheated."

"It's not like that. It's just that I'm not that interesting," I laughed

"Tell me about your family."

"Well, to be honest, I haven't seen my parents in almost twenty years. They died in a car accident while I was in...."

"While you were in?" Luke asked, looking at me skeptically. He looked at me like he knew I had almost said too much. Like he knew I was trying to hide something from him.

"While I was in Vegas. I moved there right out of high school. And I haven't talked to the rest of my family since I left."

"Sorry to hear about your parents. Has to be tough, growing up without them in your life."

"It was, but I made it. How about we talk about something else? My parents is my sore spot."

"Yeah. Cool. So, how did you get into the sex industry? Did you get introduced into that while living in Vegas?"

"Yes and no. I didn't get into the sex industry until a couple years ago when I got my windfall. But I learned the sex industry was lucrative during my stay in Vegas."

"You ever strip?" he asked, raising a brow.

"No. I don't like to shake my ass for money. I like being in the background."

"Do you like women?"

I was taken aback. "What kind of question is that?"

"Well, considering your industry and the dominant personality traits you have, I thought I would ask. I didn't mean to offend you." He didn't look sorry.

"It's okay. I'm not offended." I said, tossing away any reservations about discussing sex. Men talked about sex like they talked about sports. I was going to show him I could get on his level. "I think women are beautiful, and I play around

95

with them every now and then. But a relationship with a woman is a no-no. I'm not into relationships. They are complicated."

"Amen to that. Ever been in love?"

I had a hard time answering that question. "Yes. A long time ago."

"Me, too. A long time ago," he sighed.

Silence engulfed us. For the first time since our evening began, we were at a loss for words. I had also lost my appetite.

"Hey, you wanna go for a walk?" Luke asked, throwing his napkin onto the table.

"Yes. I'll get the waiter," I said, about to raise my hand and signal our need for service.

Luke grabbed my hand to stop me. "I got it."

He continued holding my hand as he signaled the waitress heading in our direction. I tried to pull my hand away, but he held it tight. "Would you bring me the check, please. We are ready to leave," he told the young white woman who approached our table.

When she walked away, I snatched my hand away from him. "What the hell was that about?"

He wore a smug smile. "I'm old fashioned. My father taught me to be chivalrous."

"Well, I'll get the bill since I picked the restaurant," I said as I searched my Gucci tote for my platinum card. I knew that chivalry line was bullshit. He was one-upping me.

"Syncere, relax. You don't have to fight me for power. Why can't you be the woman and let me be the man?"

I looked up and seen him probing me with his intense stare. "Because I'm not your woman and you're not my man. You work for me, remember?"

"Our business relationship is not in question. Rather, our

roles as man and woman. As the man, I'm taking responsibility for our meal. Chivalry."

"Bullshit. You're only 27 years old, but you sound old as hell. Luke, I'm 38 and fully capable as a woman and entrepreneur of taking care of myself. I pay for my own food, buy my own clothes, pay my own bills."

"And you love to dominate people every chance you get. Can't let somebody who enjoys being around you show you a good time, huh?"

I didn't have a legitimate response for that. For the last seventeen years of my life I was forced by circumstances to develop a dominant personality. I had to put on my Boss Bitch persona because it kept me from being vulnerable. Kept me alive. "I'm not used to being around someone like you. You're different," I said humbly as I closed up my purse.

Luke was different. Rare. A unique combination of brains, confidence, drive, and manliness. He was the first man I met who was on my level in every area. That frightened and excited me.

"I'll take that as a compliment," he smiled as he handed the waitress his credit card when she popped back up with the bill. When she walked away, he gave me a wink, continuing to wear his cocky smile. A victory smile.

After we left the restaurant, we walked a few blocks, talking and enjoying the summer night. Luke was growing on me by the minute. I liked his swagger. He was a man's man. And as we walked, he kept his chivalry on full display. He kept his hand at my lower back and walked on the traffic side of the sidewalk. As we headed back toward the restaurant's parking lot, I found myself not wanting our evening to end.

"You didn't win anything," I told him as we walked

toward my car.

"Who said anything about winning?" he asked, smiling down at me.

He knew what I was talking about. I knew it. "I can read your mind. I know what you're thinking."

Suddenly and unexpectedly, he grabbed me, spinning me around to face him as he forced me against my car. His spontaneous aggression turned me on. I hadn't been manhandled like that in a long time.

"What am I thinking right now?" he asked, pressing his body into mine, his lips hovering inches from my lips.

I wanted to close the distance between our mouths, but I knew he wanted me to do it. I knew it was a power thing. He wanted me to initiate contact. Probably trying to get back at me for not giving him my number when we met at Joey's. I decided I would play his game, but I upped the ante.

"You're thinking about how badly you want to know if my lips taste as good as they look," I said huskily, my voice dripping with sexiness.

"You must be kin to Dionne Warwick," he said, brushing his bottom lip against mine.

Our eye contact remained strong as he slid his hands down my body and rested them on my hips. The mood was so erotic. I was about to give in and suck his bottom lip into my mouth when he caved first.

Yes!

Kissing Luke set off explosions inside of me like someone had detonated tiny bombs all over my body. He was a great kisser. His lips were soft and his tongue was warm and juicy. It danced against mine like they were doing an Argentine Tango. I dug my hands inside his suit jacket and ran my hand along his shoulders and back. The feel of his muscles got my juices flowing. And when he ground his pelvis into my stomach, letting me feel what was between his legs, I knew I was going wherever he wanted me to go.

"Stay with me tonight," he groaned, breaking the kiss.

"Okay," I nodded, going for his lips again.

And then my phone rang.

"Mm, wait. Let me get this."

He backed away and began watching me. His stare was seductive.

"What is it?" I answered.

"Syn, you gotta get here. Some local rap niggas just got into it with some ball players. Bryce and Bone in the middle, trying to break it up."

All the feminine vulnerability I had been feeling vanished when I heard the distress in Jayda's voice. "Okay. I'll be there in about ten minutes."

"What's up?" Luke asked after I hung up.

"I gotta get to my club. A fight broke out."

"I'm coming with you," Luke said, about to get in the car.

"No, Luke. I got this. This is business," I said as I climbed behind the steering wheel.

"But, Syncere, ain't no telling–"

"I got it!" I snapped. The erotic power jockeying was gone. My money was on the line. "I can take care of myself. Thanks for dinner. I'll call you."

Luke stood outside my door like he expected me to say something else. I had no more words. I had to take care of business. I didn't even look up at him as I pulled out of the parking space. I couldn't. I had to focus.

But right before I turned out of the parking lot, I checked my rearview mirror. Luke stood in the same spot, watching me drive away.

I hated leaving him like I did, but as I drove toward my

club, I couldn't help but think how Jayda's call was right on time. Luke had some kind of magical hold on me. Around him, I was too soft. Too feminine. Too vulnerable. And while those feelings felt good in those moments, I knew I couldn't submerge myself in them. I had to continue to be sharp, focused, aloof, and even cold at times. I knew I could lose myself in Luke like I had with my first love. I couldn't let that happen again. Losing myself in a man had cost me everything I used to be and everything I used to love. I couldn't let that happen again.

***

"What happened?" I asked when I walked into my club. The bright lights were up and all the customers were gone. A few dancers were using brooms to sweep up piles of broken glass. There was also a pile of broken furniture and what looked like blood spots in the middle of the club.

"Them li'l bitch-ass Dirty Boys got mad 'cause the ball players was takin' all the girls," Bone said, his muscles twitching.

Bone was a big man. An ex-body builder, he was 6'8" and weighed almost 250 pounds. He was dark-skinned, bald headed, had no neck, and muscles everywhere. He looked like he lived in the gym and ate the weights.

"Where is Bryce?" I asked as I assessed the damage. It didn't look too bad. A few tables and chairs.

"Nobody got hurt but Bryce. Got hit by a flying bottle. He left for the hospital a few minutes ago. Wasn't that bad. Got his hand cut up."

"Did anybody call the police?" I asked, hoping they didn't. The last thing I needed was police contact.

"Nah, wasn't no need. Me and Bryce got to slingin'

niggas around like rag dolls, and that shit died down as soon as it started."

"Okay. Cool. Thanks for being here," I said, giving my Incredible Hulk a pat on the arm.

"No problem, boss lady. That's what you pay me for."

"Where is Jayda?" I asked as I headed for my office.

"I think she in your office or in the back with the girls."

When I walked in my office, Jayda was sitting at my desk using the phone. Jayda was my friend and club manager. I ran a tight ship and overseen almost every aspect of The Den of Syn. Jayda was my eyes and ears when I wasn't around or needed to delegate some responsibilities. And she was good at her job. She knew how to separate business from pleasure.

"Okay. I'll call you later. I have to go," she said before hanging up the phone.

"Bone filled me in on everything. Them dirty-ass niggas ain't allowed in here no more," I said as I sat down in one of the chairs in front of my desk.

"So, what do you want to do? Are we opening back up, or what?" she asked, staring at me through eyes that looked like they had gone through war. And they had. Her war came in the form of a ten-year prison bid.

"I think I'ma close for the night. Gotta get that shit cleaned up and replace the tables and chairs."

"Okay. I'll tell the girls," she said, getting up to leave.

"Wait," I stopped her. "How many girls out there?"

"Nine. It's Thursday."

"Here. Give them $200 apiece. I know they won't like hearing I closed the doors for the night," I said as I walked over to my wall safe. I counted off $1,800 and gave it to her.

When Jayda left, I sat down on the couch and began replaying my evening with Luke. I hated leaving him the way I had. I wanted to call him and apologize and make sure everything was okay, but I couldn't bring myself to pick up the phone. My pride wouldn't let me. But I did wish I would have hit that. Just thinking about how his body felt against mine turned me on and got me wet.

"Okay. I gave them the news. They didn't like it, but they understood. Need anything else?" Jayda said as she walked into my office.

I gave her the once-over as she stood before me. Jayda wasn't fine, but she had that sex appeal thing on lock. She wore her hair in a short, silver afro. She had dark chocolate, flawless skin, a juicy top lip, and a nicely-toned, athletic body. And one of the meatiest pussies I had ever sucked. She wasn't a lesbian and had a man at home, but we messed around whenever I was in the mood.

"Yeah. Lock the door," I said, looking over her tight denim shorts, gray halter top, and high heels.

"Ooh! What do you want me to do?" she asked as she sashayed over to lock the door.

"Grab my strap-on from the drawer."

"Oh, hell no, Syn. Not tonight. Last time you fucked me with that thing, Devin swore I cheated on him. That shit stretched me out."

"I want you to fuck me," I told her as I took off my dress and threw it on the chair.

Hearing that I wanted her to do me changed her tone. "Ooh, what has gotten into you? You never let me fuck you before."

And I hadn't. Every time we messed around, I was in control. I had a thing about a woman being in control of me when I had sex. I didn't allow that. "I'm in the mood for something new," I told her as I slipped off my panties and bra and lay back on the couch.

The smile never left Jayda's face as she strapped on the big, black snake. "I'ma enjoy this shit."

"Be aggressive. Like a man."

"A'ight, bitch," she said in a deep voice as she knelt between my legs. She began by sucking my nipples.

I didn't want foreplay, though, so I grabbed the head of the strap-on and stuck it inside me, then grabbed her ass cheeks. I wanted some dick! "Oh, shit! Damn!" I moaned when she started moving her hips. I had never had anything that big inside of me. I felt it in my stomach.

I had to put my hand against her pelvis to stop her from going too deep. But, playing the man's role, she wrestled my hand away and went deeper. "Oh, fuck!" I moaned, grabbing handfuls of the back of her shirt as she long-stroked me.

Right when it felt like I was about to cum, she stopped. "Turn around. Doggy style," she ordered.

I did as I was told. Jayda got behind me and began working that piece of plastic like she was born with it. I pictured Luke's hands on my hips and his pelvis slamming into my ass. By the time my orgasm built back up, I had lost myself in my fantasy.

"Oh yeah, Luke! I'm about to cum, baby!" I screamed as I slammed my ass back at Jayda.

When I came, it was intense and seemed to last forever. My body tingled as I fell forward onto the couch. I felt good all over. And relaxed. And calm.

"So, who is Luke?" Jayda asked, ruining my moment.

Chapter 13

"Daddy, will you be at my daddy/daughter dance next week?" Latia asked, looking across the table at me with eyes that begged me not to turn her down.

"Wouldn't miss it for the world, baby."

And I wouldn't. My daughter meant the world to me. Having her love and approval superseded everything in my life. And I planned on cutting it up with her at the dance being hosted by Shay's mother's church.

"Good. Can you buy me a new dress? I want to wear something new."

"Yeah. How about we dress in the same colors. But I ain't wearing pink," I warned.

Latia laughed a cute laugh that made my heart flutter. "Okay, Daddy. You don't have to wear pink. But what about purple?" she snickered.

"What!"

"I'm just playing, Daddy. How about white?"

"Now you're talking. I can't believe you asked your Daddy to wear purple. You lucky I don't jack-knife power bomb you in that garbage can," I teased.

"Puh-lease, Daddy! You know better," she sassed.

That was my baby!

After leaving the Culver's restaurant, I drove over to the Mid-Town Shopping Plaza to get Latia a dress and a pair of shoes for the dance. I loved spending time with my baby girl. We went out regularly. I did this not only because I loved spending time with her, but I also wanted to show her what a real man was like. I had to combat all the bullshit she picked up from her mother and Pistol.

When we left the strip mall with Latia's new dress and shoes, I decided to take her home. It was almost eight o'clock, and I needed to have her in the house by her nine o'clock curfew. Plus, I had to get some sleep. I was meeting with a new client in the morning, and I wanted to do some more research on a few investment opportunities before I went to bed.

"Daddy, when you gon' get a girlfriend?" Latia asked, catching me off guard with the question.

"Why you ask me that?" I asked, looking over at her as I pulled up to the stoplight.

"Because I never seen you with a girlfriend. Mommy got Pistol, but you don't have nobody. Why?"

I thought about how to answer her question, wondering if I should give her my 'I only want women as friends' speech. But as I looked into her precious eyes, I knew I couldn't tell her that. She took my words as serious as Christians took the words in the Bible, and the last thing I needed her doing was adopting my belief and only having boys as friends. I definitely didn't want my daughter getting around.

"I date a little bit. I just haven't found the right woman yet."

"Who are you dating right now? What's her name?"

I said the first name that came to mind. "Syncere."

"I like that name. Is she pretty?"

A visual of Syncere flashed in my mind. "Yeah. She's pretty."

"Well, maybe she can be the one, Daddy. Then you can have you somebody like Mommy does."

"Yeah. Maybe."

I turned onto Shay's block a few minutes later, and the first thing I noticed was Pistol's black Suburban parked halfway on the sidewalk. I got a strange feeling in my gut.

"Wait right here," I told Latia as I climbed out of my truck. I walked up on the sidewalk, and before I could get to the porch I heard the sound of a heated argument coming from the house. Pistol was yelling about something, and Shay was yelling back. I thought about leaving. I wanted to pull away and keep Latia for the night, but when I heard Shay scream, I ran into the house.

They were in the living room, on the floor. Shay was on her back with Pistol on top of her, pinning her down. Pistol's face was scratched and bleeding. Shay's nose was bloody.

"Aye, y'all! Chill this shit!" I yelled, grabbing Pistol off Shay.

"Getcho hands off me, fuck-nigga!" Pistol yelled, pushing me away.

I stumbled backward. Since I didn't come for a fight, I didn't respond to the shove. I turned to Shay. "Shay, y'all gotta chill this shit. Latia is outside. She don't need to see this shit."

"Don't come in my shit tellin' me what to do. You don't live here, nigga," Pistol cut in.

I looked over at him with a 'nigga, please' look. He stared back at me with the meanest look he could muster. His hands were clenched into fists.

"Listen, man. I didn't come in here to fight you. I'm trynna bring Latia home. But I'm not lettin' her in here if y'all on this bullshit. And I'm not Shay, Pistol. I hit back."

I watched Pistol's jaw clench and muscles spasm. He telegraphed the punch, and I was ready for him. I dodged the wild haymaker and landed a quick 2-piece to his jaw. The punches were stiff jabs, not intended to knock him out. I just wanted to let him know I could knuckle up.

Pistol stumbled back a little bit before catching his balance. Then he threw up his dukes. I threw up mine.

"Luke, stop!" Shay screamed.

I looked over at her like she was crazy. I couldn't believe

she was screaming at me when Pistol swung first.

And in the split second it took me to give her the evil eye, Pistol struck. He swung another wild haymaker, and I didn't have time to dodge it like I had the first one. I was able to move my face just enough so he missed my chin, but caught my cheekbone. It burned. I knew his knuckles had cut me.

When we got back into our boxer stances, he smiled at me. Apparently he thought he had done something. I showed him he hadn't when I tore into his ass like a lion on a wildebeest. Left, right, left, right, upper-cut. Just like I had been practicing since I was twelve. Pistol was out cold.

"Get the fuck outta my house, Luke!" Shay yelled as she ran to Pistol's side.

I stood over Pistol's unconscious body and looked down at Shay with disgust as she tried to comfort and wake him. I wanted to punch her. Pistol had just beat her up and attacked me, yet she was cursing me out and trying to comfort him. It was hard to believe we were once in love. She was lucky Pop taught me not to hit women.

"Stupid-ass, bitch!" I muttered as I walked toward the door.

Chapter 14

"Well, I hope to God the other man got the worst of it, 'cause if you look like that and you won, he must be fucked up!" Syncere cracked and burst out laughing. She had spent the last few minutes ribbing me about the cut Pistol left on my cheek a couple days ago.

"When I left, he was still on the floor," I bragged, sitting back in my chair. I liked spending time with Syncere. She was just as cool as she was sexy. But what I didn't like were all of her jokes about my cheek. I knew I had to get her back, and I knew just the dig.

"Golden Gloves, huh? Did you get those gloves out of a gumball machine?" she cracked, laughing again.

"Yeah, laugh it up, Sheryle Underwood," I chuckled, taking my shot.

At the mentioning of the popular black comedian, Syncere stopped laughing and looked offended. "Why you gotta call me her?" she frowned.

I laughed harder. "You crazy, Syncere."

"That's my girl, but damn. Why not Symone or Kim Whitley? Somebody light-skinned. I ain't that black."

"Yeah, now I know yo' kryptonite. Keep talkin' shit."

"Whatever. So, what happened with your daughter? Did she go home with you?"

"Yeah. Her mom called me the next morning and had me drop her off before I went to work. Pistol was gone."

"Sounds like you and your daughter are close."

"We are. That's my girl. Only woman who will ever have all of my heart."

"Hmph," Syncere smirked.

I gave her the eye. "What was that?"

"What? Nothing," she smiled, eyeing me as she took a

sip of her Merlot.

I held her stare. Syncere was fine. Not cute-fine, but sexy-fine. Her light brown irises were smoky and smoldering inside her slightly slanted eyes. She had the kind of lips that could do things to a man to make him say her name. Her hair was long, thick, and curly. Her skin had a glow and looked softer than cotton. And her body? Mm, mm, mm! If she would have been the stripper instead of the strip club owner, she probably would've made enough money to buy the club. And the tight, red dress she wore showed it all.

Syncere intrigued the hell out of me. She was a powerful woman. A go-getter. Strong minded. Driven. I had never seen anything like her. She was tough as nails, but feminine, too. Sometimes she made plays for power and control, and I liked that. The challenge. The game. And I liked beating her. I recognized all of her tricks, knew what she was up to. And I knew if a man showed her any weakness, she would chew him up and spit him out. I definitely didn't plan on being anyone's meal.

"What?" she asked, setting her glass down.

I had been so caught up in admiring her I got caught staring. I knew I had to think of something. "Do you know your eyes betray you?"

She looked at me like I had just told her I was selling tickets to the moon. "What are you talking about, Luke?"

"I know you try to be an ice queen sometimes. In control. You play for it. And while you are a strong sistah, your vulnerability shows in your eyes."

"Is that right, Luke?" she asked, sitting back in her chair.

I sat forward, my elbows on the table, my hands clenched under my chin. "That's what I see."

"You are wrong, Luke. Very perceptive, but wrong."

I knew I was right.

"And do you want me to tell you what I see?" she asked, peering at me like she was trying to turn me into stone.

"Do tell."

"A good-looking, over-confidant man who is used to getting his way with women. But, when a woman takes the lead, you can't handle it. It is a blow to your ego to let a woman take charge. So, you fight it. Always get the last word. Have to pay for the meals. Acting chivalrous. Not only do you want control, but you also want to look like you're in control. You can't take a back seat to anyone, especially a woman."

The chess match had begun and she had just made a power move.

"You know why I fight it?" I asked.

She gave me a silent yes by lifting her eyebrows.

"Because it's not natural. God created you from me for me. A man's natural position is the head. The leader. The problem with our community is there are not enough men in their God-given positions. Boys don't know what men look like, so they grow to be thugs. Girls don't know what men look like, so they take control of the house just like their mothers did. And then, if by some chance that girl meets a man, she will fight him for his God-given position every chance she gets."

"This is not the days of Jesus. We live in a day and age where women are just as capable as men. Just as able. Just as strong. Men's monopoly on power is shrinking. We are equals. And, in some cases, superior."

"Equal as human beings, superior in nurturing, but inferior in authority, Syncere."

"I am independent. I have my own authority, Luke."

"Independence can't satisfy your cravings for a strong touch. Independence doesn't keep you warm at night.

Independence doesn't give you a family or make your house a home. Independence doesn't complete you. The only thing independence does is drive a wedge between you and your man by trying to convince you that you don't need him. And the difference between a man and a woman is men know we need women. This is a man's world, but it wouldn't be nothing without a woman or girl. And we're not afraid to admit that."

Syncere became silent. Check.

"You want to get out of here?" I asked, trying to hide my smile.

"Yes," she said demurely.

I signaled the waiter.

***

"You are different," Syncere mumbled as we walked toward her car.

"What do you mean?"

"What you say. How you say it. The way you carry yourself. The way you make me act around you. If my girls ever see me with you, they wouldn't even recognize me. I can best everybody. Except you. I never heard that independence stance explained to me like that. But now that I think about it, it makes perfect sense. Our independence is tearing up our homes."

"Wanna know where I learned that?"

"Do tell."

"A book. I read it in college. *From Dust To The Age of Full Strength.*"

"I might have to order that. Be ready for you next time," she teased.

Silence engulfed us as we closed the distance to her car. I

didn't want to let her go.

"So, what now?" Syn asked, stopping at her driver's side door and staring up at me. The moonlight shone in her eyes as she looked up at me. I could see her desire for me written all over her face. She didn't want our night to end, either.

"I say we do what feels good. What feels right." I took my own advice and bent down to kiss her. Her lips tasted like honey, and her tongue tasted like wine. I was instantly intoxicated.

She let out a sexy moan as she wrapped her arms around the back of my neck. My hands felt up her body, eventually landing and resting on her pretty, round rear. Her cheeks felt like cotton wrapped in silk.

I would have stood in that parking lot kissing her all night, but Givenchy was demanding attention. "Where are your keys?" I asked after I came up for air.

Syncere stood there, staring at me like she was in a trance, When she snapped back to reality, she opened her purse and gave me her car keys. I popped the locks, opened the door, and sat her in the driver's seat before racing around to the other side. I wasn't even concerned with my truck that sat a parking space over. Syncere was hot and ready. That truck could wait 'til morning. I knew she couldn't.

"Where do you want to go?" she asked after I climbed in.

"Your place."

During the drive to her crib, I kept her on fire with licks, kisses, and touches. When we pulled up to her house in the Glendale suburb, I had her panties up to my nose, taking big sniffs while my fingers worked her lower lips.

After she parked in her driveway, she wasted no time attacking me.

"Wait, Syncere. Hold up." I stopped her. I didn't want to have sex with her yet. I was about to pull a play for power.

All of it.

"What?" she paused, her face showing a mix between lust and alarm.

I reached for the keys she left in the ignition as I opened my door. "Let's go inside."

"You're doing this on purpose. You're wrong, Luke," she sulked as she climbed off of me.

Check.

I followed the swaying of Syncere's hips across her driveway and onto her porch. After unlocking the door, she busied herself with the alarm while I looked around. Her living room was decorated regally. Two high-back, throne-like chairs sat a few feet from an electric fireplace. Between the fireplace and the chairs was a giant, white polar bear skin rug. The floors were polished hardwood. A few African paintings and sculptures decorated the room, and a giant cream-colored couch was parked underneath a picture window.

"What do you have to drink?" I asked as I looked around.

"I'll be right back. Make yourself comfortable."

While she busied herself with whatever she was doing, I went over to turn on the fireplace.

"You even know how to work a state-of-the-art fireplace. I'm impressed," Syncere called from behind me.

I spun around and seen her walking toward me with a bottle of Patron and two glasses. "Mm. Good choice. Why don't we sit in front of the fire?" I suggested, taking the liquor and glasses.

"A romantic, huh? Jack of all trades, are you, Luke?" she asked as we sat on the bear rug.

"I do a li'l something-something," I smiled as I poured our drinks. I gave her a glass and kept my own. "Did I ever tell you that you have a pretty name? I like Syncere. How you spell it is unique."

"Yeah. It is unique. But the people close to me call me Syn."

"Syn, huh? I wonder why?" I chuckled, running my hand up her thigh.

"If I told you, I would have to kill you." Syncere looked sinful under the glow of the fire. She oozed sex appeal. "How many women do you have, Luke?"

I took a sip of my drink before answering. "None."

"No, seriously. It's not a big deal. I just want to know."

"I don't have any women. Honestly. But, I do have friends. Quite a few."

"Are you feeling any of them."

"Yeah. One."

"Who?"

"You."

"Stop playing, Luke."

"I'm serious as cancer."

We became silent as we took sips of our drinks and listened to the fire crackle.

"What about you? How many friends do you have?"

"I have no one. Just tossed the guy I had. He was weak."

"What about women?"

"I don't mess with women like that. I only play with them when I'm in the mood."

"How do you feel now?"

"Like playing."

I stuck my finger into my drink and then brought my liquor-dipped digit to her lips. She wrapped her lips around my finger and swallowed it like she was deep-throating. And then, for good measure, she moved her lips up and down the length of my finger a few times. Givenchy sprang to attention.

I pulled my finger from her mouth and tongued her down. We sat our drinks on the floor as I laid her on the rug. When I pulled the straps of her dress down past her shoulders, two big, brown globes spilled out like a chocolate avalanche. I wasted no time sucking one of her nipples into my mouth.

"Ooh!" she moaned, arching her back as I teased her nipple with my tongue. It got hard as a diamond.

I teased the other one for a while before moving on. I planted kisses down the length of her torso until I found her Wonderland. After spreading her legs wide, I inhaled deeply. She smelled great. Like peaches.

"Mm, Luke!" she moaned, rubbing my head as I placed a few kisses on her inner thighs.

After a few more teasing kisses, I moved my lips over a few inches until I was hovering over her sex. I didn't touch her, but I could see and feel a chill of anticipation run through her body. She was ready.

I began by licking circles around her outer lips. She squirmed like a worm on a fishing hook. After licking a few circles, I began moving my tongue up and down from her clit to her hole. She went wild when I stuck my tongue into her hole and began moving it back and forth. She grabbed the back of my head and began humping my face. And right when she was on the brink of an orgasm, I removed my tongue from her hole and started licking circles around her lips again. I repeated the process a few times, licking circles around her outer lips, licking up and down her clit, and then sticking my tongue in and out of her hole. Every time she was about to cum, I slowed down and started licking circles around her lips again.

"Please, Luke. Make me cum," she begged. Check.

I couldn't suppress my grin if I wanted to. And I didn't.

But what I did want to do was make her cum. I put my lips around her clit and sucked it like it was the best piece of candy I had ever tasted. When she came, her body stiffened and she grabbed my head and began shivering like she was freezing.

"Ooh, shit, Luke! Ah!"

When her orgasm passed, I stood to undress. Syn stared up at me like I was a God. After I took off my boxers, Givenchy stood to attention like a flag pole. Syn looked at my meat like it was the best thing she had ever seen in her life as she licked her lips. I wanted to feel those lips around my pole. Really bad. But the taste and smell of what she had between her thighs had me dying to be inside of her, so I dove in.

We both moaned as I entered her. Her walls felt like thousand-count sheets to a homeless man. And I tangled myself in them. I had Syncere in every position. I gave it to her good, hard, and long, Gave her everything I had. Dominated her. And when we fell asleep on the rug afterward, she clung to me like an infant to its mother.

Checkmate!

Chapter 15

I watched the house for signs of movement as I pulled my sports car to the curb. I could see the lights were on, but I couldn't see inside because the curtains were drawn. Throwing caution to the wind, I grabbed my purse, leaving the car running as I left. I would make this quick.

I trotted up the steps, trying to be as quiet as possible as I pulled the brown envelope from my purse. After dropping the package in the black matte mailbox, I turned to leave. I got one foot on the stairs when I heard something that made me stop in my tracks. I walked back toward the door and pressed my ear against it. My pulse thudded in my ear as I listened.

"Stop playin' wit' me, Trinity! Where it at?" a man yelled.

"I don't have it. Let me go, A.J.!" the woman screamed.

"I ain't playin' wit' cho ass! Gimme the muthafuckin' money!"

"Stop hitting me, A.J.! Stop!"

Oh, no he ain't!

I pulled my .380 from my purse and tried the door. It was unlocked. I barged into that house like I had a search warrant, gun aimed high and ready to shoot. The sitting room was empty. "Trinity!" I called as I began to search the house.

"Who the fuck is you, and what ch'all doin' in my house?" A.J. asked, appearing from the hallway. He looked me up and down aggressively, but when he seen the gun in my hand, a flash of fear shown in his eyes.

"Where is Trinity?" I asked, noticing the wrinkling of his white t-shirt and the stretching of his collar.

"Ay, you that lady that was at the door a couple of weeks ago. I told you, yo' friend don't live here. Get the fuck out!"

I didn't budge. "Where is Trinity?"

"Who are you, and how do you know my name?" Trinity asked, appearing from the same hallway A.J. had.

Looking at her took my breath away. I could feel my emotions rising. I could feel the tears welling up in my eyes, but I fought off my emotions. Danger was present. "Are you okay?" I asked, looking her over for injuries. Her clothes were a bit disheveled and a bruise was forming on her throat.

"I'm fine. Who are you?" she asked, looking back and forth from my face to my gun.

"I'm a friend. Did he hit you?"

"We had an–"

"Don't talk to this bitch. Get the fuck out!" A.J. yelled.

"Come with me, Trinity. You don't need this," I said, reaching out my hand to her.

"She ain't goin' nowhere wit' chu, bitch. Now get the fuck out!" A.J. yelled.

I was tired of him calling me out of my name. "Call me another bitch and I'ma blow yo' li'l dick off!" I threatened, pointing my gun at his crotch.

He stepped away from Trinity and covered himself with both hands.

"Come with me, Trinity. This is not love, baby. You don't have to stay in this," I pleaded, tearing up as I reached my hand out to her.

I could see the confusion in her eyes when she looked back at me. I was a stranger and I had a gun. I knew she could hear the compassion in my voice and see the love in my eyes, but she didn't budge.

"You can trust me, Trinity. I swear I won't hurt you. I'm a friend."

After a few more moments of hesitation, she reached out her hand to me.

"Hell nah, bitch!" I heard A.J. yell.

I turned my head just in time to see him rushing toward me. I tried to shoot him, but he tackled me before I could raise my gun. I landed on my back. He was on top of me.

"A.J., stop!" Trinity screamed.

"Punk-ass bitch! Gimme dis gun!" A.J. yelled as he tried to wrestle the gun from my hand.

He was almost twenty years younger and a lot stronger than I was. I was losing the battle for my gun, and I knew if I let him take it, he would shoot me. So, I went for every man's weakness.

"Aw, shit!" he groaned, loosening his grip on my gun as he reached for his balls. I had kneed him so hard I tried to push his nuts into his stomach.

"You fucking coward!" I screamed as I pistol-whipped him across the face. When he rolled off me, I sprang to my feet. "You like to hit women, huh?" I screamed as I kicked him in the face with the pointed tip of my Ferragamo boot.

He groaned in pain, using one hand to clutch his now-bleeding face while the other clutched his busted balls.

"Lady, please!" Trinity cried, begging me to stop. I ignored her.

"Coward-ass motherfucker! Get the fuck out of here. If I ever see your ass again, I will kill you!"

He crawled toward the door slowly. I opened it up for him and used my foot to give him a push.

"Who are you?" Trinity asked after I closed the door.

"I am a friend. My name is Syncere," I told her as I put away my gun.

Trinity looked at me with a mix of awe and fear on her face. "A friend of who? How do you know me?"

"It's complicated, and I can't make much sense of it now, but you can trust me. I want to help you."

I could see the question in her eyes. I wanted to put her at ease, but I didn't have enough time to explain it all. Nor was I ready. "Why were you fighting?" I asked, shifting the attention away from me.

"Over money. Somebody drops money in my mailbox almost ever month. A thousand or more. I normally give it to him because I don't know where it comes from and I don't want to be responsible for it, but I needed the money to pay some bills and rent. But he wanted it. So we fought."

"Well, you don't have to give him any more money. That money is from a friend of your parents. They–"

"You know who my parents are?"

Shit! I had said too much.

"Um, not exactly. But I know that money is for you. I've been giving it to you."

"Really? Why didn't you give it to me personally? Why were you always dropping it off?"

"Because I wanted to remain anonymous. Look, I can't get into all of that right now. Not at this time. I will explain it all later. I promise."

"But I don't understand," she whined.

"You will. Later. But I have to go," I said, turning and walking toward the door.

She followed. "Will I see you again? Do you have a number?"

I reached into my pocket and pulled out my business card. "Here is my card. Call me if you need anything. I mean anything at all."

"Okay," she mumbled.

I could see the questions swirling around in her mind as she took my card. I wanted to pull her into my bosom and tell her everything, but I couldn't. I didn't know how. I didn't know where to start.

"Stay away from A.J. He doesn't love you. Get a real man. A man won't take advantage of you. He will give you the advantage. This is a man's world, but it wouldn't be nothing without a woman or a girl. A real man will help you. Complete you."

"Okay," she mumbled.

"I meant what I said. Stay away from A.J. And if I see him again, I'm shooting him."

"Okay," she smiled.

I didn't believe her. I knew she was going to see him again.

"Alright. Give me a hug. I have to go," I said, opening my arms to receive her.

When she wrapped her arms around me, I wanted to cry.

"Thanks, Syncere."

"No, problem. And, by the way, there is something in your mailbox."

Chapter 16

It took everything inside of me to keep my emotions in check until I got to my car, and as soon as I closed the door and stuck the key in the ignition, the tears came. I couldn't stop them from flowing. That was the first time I had been in Trinity's presence since she was six months old. Looking into her face and staring into her eyes had touched me. She looked so much like her father. I had missed her whole life. I wanted to tell her who I was, but I couldn't bring myself to do it. I was scared. Scared she would never forgive me. So, instead of leveling with her, I decided to just be there for her in any and every way I could.

I didn't even remember the drive to my club, but after I pulled into my parking space, my phone began to vibrate. I wiped the tears from my face as I picked up my phone. My heart fluttered when I recognized the number.

"Hey, Luke."

"Hey. How are you? Is everything okay? You sound down."

"I've had a challenging day, but I'm okay. Nothing I can't handle."

"Being Wonder Woman again, huh?"

"More like Super Woman. Get it right. You heard Alicia Keys."

"Okay, Super Woman. Do you have time for supper?"

Visions of the night Luke spent at my house flashed in my mind. I could feel the heat from the fireplace and the soft fur of the bear rug.

"I have to be at the club all night. Can I take a rain check?"

"What's so special about tonight that you can't leave? Don't you have managers or something?"

"I do have a manager, but I still need to be here. A big magazine guy is throwing a party in about an hour. I have to be here for that."

"Oh. I see. Well, how about I come to see you?"

"Luke, I can't ask you to do that. I'll be really busy, and I won't have a chance to really hang with you."

"I'm sure I can find a few of your employees to entertain me until you're available," he laughed.

I didn't like the thought of anyone entertaining him. "Funny, Luke."

"No, but seriously, I can't get the night I spent with you out of my mind. I have to see you. Don't make me beg."

Visions of him teasing me popped into my mind. I had never wanted to cum so bad in my life. "I should make you beg since you made me."

"I ain't too proud to beg."

"Beg, Luke."

"Please, baby."

"That's it?" I asked, feeling cheated.

"I ain't Keith Sweat, girl. That's all I got."

Now, that was funny.

"Okay. C'mon. I can't wait to see you."

When I walked into my club, it was a packed house, just as I expected. Stuntin' 4-Eva Magazine was throwing their launch party, and everybody who was somebody was up in the place. I normally had about ten girls working weeknights, but tonight I had twenty. Big money was in the house, and I wanted to tap those pockets.

I stopped over by the bar to check the scene. My girls were walking the floor in different levels of dress, and the men were salivating over them, a few of them making it rain. I knew we would clean up tonight.

"Yo, Syn!"

I looked around the dimly-lit room to see who had called my name. My eyes landed on a dark-skinned stranger in an olive-green suit who was getting up from a table.

"Syncere, my name is Terrance Jackson, but everyone calls me J-Rock," he introduced himself, extending a hand.

"Hi, J-Rock. Nice to meet you," I smiled as I shook his hand.

"The pleasure is all mine's, really. But, listen, I have a business deal I want to run by you. I have an up-and-coming local artist who is about to blow. Li'l Laya. Heard of him?"

I thought for a few moments. "Yeah. I've heard of him."

"Good. Well, we shootin' a video, and I seen a few girls I would like to shoot. I approached them, but they told me to run it by you."

"No soliciting. Club policy," I agreed. "Do you have a card? A way for me to reach you?"

"Sure," he said, reaching into the breast pocket of his suit and pulling out a business card.

"Listen, can we talk about this tomorrow? Tonight is a busy night, and I won't be able to give you my undivided attention."

"Yeah. Tomorrow's cool. I know Travis from Stuntin' 4-Eva is gon' be in the place, and I wanted to get in a word before you became unavailable."

"Okay. Nice to meet you J-Rock. Enjoy the night," I said, giving him another handshake before turning toward my office.

I had only taken a few steps when I noticed someone watching me. I looked to my left and locked eyes with a very good looking, light-skinned man. He wore a stark white suit. In the club's dim lighting, he stood out like a female inmate in an all-male prison. His face looked familiar, but I wasn't sure where I had seen him. Nor did I dwell on it. I wanted to get in my office and change before Travis and his crew showed up. I had to look good for my photo ops!

After letting myself into my office, I closed the door, went over to the small closet, and pulled out my peach Georgina Chapman skirt suit. I had just finished changing when there was a knock at my door. "Come in," I called as I slipped on my pearl-colored red bottoms.

"A man named Calico wants to meet with you," Jayda said, peeking her head into my office.

"Who the fuck is Calico?" I frowned. I had heard of the name, but I couldn't place a face with it.

"Some man in a white suit. He must be somebody, because everybody in the club treatin' him like he Future."

"Where is he now?"

"Talking to Bone. He won't let him down the hall."

I thought for a few moments. I still had a few minutes before Travis showed up. If Calico was somebody, then I probably should meet with him. "Okay. Tell Bone to let him pass."

After giving myself a once-over in the mirror, I sat behind my desk and waited for Calico. I didn't have to wait long. He rapped on the door lightly.

"Come in."

Calico walked into my office with the air of a Prime Minister or President. He stood about six feet tall and had a medium build. His tailored white suit fit him perfectly. It looked like him and P-Diddy had the same tailor. His white shoes looked like he pulled them out of the box before he walked in the club, his nails were clean and manicured, his face clean shaven, and he wore his straightened hair in a ponytail that came past his shoulders. His high yellow complexion and 'good hair' told me he was loaded. If I had to guess his age, I would've said forty, but he looked younger.

"What a mighty fine establishment, Syncere," he said, standing in the middle of my office and looking around as he adjusted his diamond cufflinks.

"Thank you, Mr. Calico. Have a seat."

He strolled across the room like he was floating on a cloud. "You know, Syncere, I've been looking forward to meeting you for quite some time."

"Is that right?" I asked, raising a brow.

"Yes. It appears we have mutual friends," he smiled. His smile was wicked and unfriendly, and he had the eyes of a snake.

"And who is that?"

"Rasheed and Rhoda."

It felt like I had been punched in the stomach. I tried to hide my shock and surprise, but I didn't know if I was doing a good job. I could feel my heart rate increase as beads of sweat began trickling from my armpits.

"Excuse me?" I managed.

"You heard me, Syncere. Or, should I say 'Loretta?'" He smiled, never blinking as his eyes bore a hole through me.

Shit! This was not good. "What do you want?" I asked, trying to keep my voice from cracking.

"You took something from Rasheed when you killed him. That was mine. Now, I don't give a fuck about that nigga being dead. If it's true he tried to rape you, then he got what he deserved. But I do need the contents of that bag. The 100K you took."

"I don't know what you're talking about." I refused to entertain what he was talking about. I didn't give a damn who he was. No way was I giving him $100,000 dollars.

"Loretta–"

"Don't call me that," I snapped.

He smiled again. "Syncere, I'm a business man, and a damned good one. Don't insult my intelligence by lying to me. You just got out of prison a little over a year ago, and you mean to tell me you created all of this on your own?" he asked, making a sweeping gesture around the room with his hand.

"I told you, I don't know what you're talking about. And I don't have your money."

He stared at me for a few moments. He was challenging me and reading me. My stare downs with Luke had prepared me for this moment. I never broke the eye contact.

"They told me you were tough, but I see that was an understatement. Problem is, the people I employ don't care about heart. I will make you an offer. I normally don't make offers to people who stole from me, but since you used to fuck with C-Money and he was a real nigga, I'll give you one. I want a 45% stake of The Den of Syn. After you pay me my money back with 60% interest, we will cut ties."

I looked at him like he was speaking Mandarin. "You must be out of your fucking mind."

Calico laughed as he stood to his feet. "Why does someone with such a pretty mouth use nasty words?"

I didn't respond. I wanted him gone.

"I will send my people to see you in a week. Hopefully we can settle this matter with diplomacy," he said before leaving my office.

"Fuck!" I swore, grabbing at my temples. Today was not my day. I couldn't believe Calico knew C-Money, Rhoda, and Rasheed. For a moment I considered paying him the money. It wasn't like I didn't have it. But I didn't like that he tried to bully me. And the 60% interest was crazy. That was a total of $160,000. No way in hell was I giving him six figures. I didn't know what I was going to do, but I wasn't about to pay. Nobody was extorting Syn.

A knock on my door interrupted my thoughts.

"Come in."

Jayda peeked her head into my office, smiling like she knew Victoria's Secret. "Luke is here."

When she mentioned his name, my insides began to bubble, but I acted nonchalant. "Send him in."

When Jayda left, I stood and tried to shake away the emotions my meetings with Trinity and Calico had stirred inside me. By the time my door opened and Luke walked into my office, I was smiling like I had won an Academy Award.

"Hey, Super Woman!" he smiled, walking toward me with open arms.

"Hey, Luke," I cooed, falling into his arms. After the embrace, I stood on my tippy-toes and kissed him like I was a desert nomad and he was water.

"Feels like you missed me," he said, squeezing me tightly.

"I did," I sang, laying my head against his chest. I felt safe there.

"Well, before we close our eyes tonight, I plan on showing you everything you missed," he mumbled, his voice vibrating through my body and making my skin tingle.

I was about to return the sweet nothing when I felt someone watching us. I looked behind Luke and seen Jayda standing in the doorway.

The look on her face showed pure awe, like she was watching Northern Lights. I knew why she wore that look. She had seen me expressing emotions and showing vulnerability. Something she had never seen before.

I cut my eyes at her, giving her the meanest look I could muster. She gave me a 'busted' smile before closing the door silently.

Chapter 17

I left work with an extra pep in my step. I felt like I was over the moon, and I owed the feeling to Syncere. Why? Because my night with her was explosive. I had sexed a lot of women in my twenty-seven years on this planet, but none of those experiences could compete with my times with Syncere.

The way she moved. The way she felt. The way she talked. Everything! Just thinking about her, I was aroused. I was fast becoming addicted to her, and I wasn't sure if that was a good or bad thing. I didn't know much about her, nor had I known her that long, but there was something about her that got to me.

I was thinking about what my daughter said about finding somebody for me.

As I crossed the parking lot to get to my truck, I thought more about Syn's personality. It was almost as if there were two people living inside of her. She had a tough as nails exterior, but on the inside she was soft and vulnerable. I recognized the tough act she put on, though. It was for protection. Someone or something had forced her to develop an icy and dominant alter ego. The woman I knew behind the mask was nothing like the woman everyone else saw. It was as if the woman on the outside protected the woman on the inside. A split personality. And I planned on seeing both of them again. Tonight.

I had made it to my truck and was about to climb inside when something caught my eye. A black '90s Grand Am with tinted windows was parked about twenty or thirty feet away from me. The car seemed out of place, so I watched it out of the corner of my eye as I unlocked my door. When the tinted window on the passenger side of the car began rolling down, I instantly noticed two things. The driver's eyes and the gun.

Pop-pop-pop-pop-pop-pop-pop-pop-pop-pop!

I dove into my truck just as the shooting started. I could hear bullets slamming into my truck and feel the glass shower me as my windows exploded from the hot lead. It seemed to take forever for the shooting to stop. Then I heard an engine rev and tires screech.

"Luke! Luke! Are you okay, man?" I heard someone call.

It was my co-worker, Matt Sorensen. I didn't respond to him. I couldn't. I was in shock. I had almost been killed.

"Luke! Luke! Talk to me, man. Are you hit?" Matt yelled as he yanked open my truck door.

I just lay across the seat, staring out the shattered windows and up at the blue sky.

"Luke! Talk to me, man," Matt said as he began running his hands up and down my body to check for bullet holes.

Feeling his touch woke me up. "I'm good. I'm okay." I shot up in my seat. Glass shards flew everywhere. I looked around the parking lot and seen other coworkers gathering around my truck.

"Holy shit! Man, I've never seen anything like that," Matt said, stepping back to look at the damage.

"Luke, what the hell was that?" asked one of the board members, Thomas Berkshire. "You okay?"

"Yeah. I'm fine. I'm okay," I reassured everyone as I stepped from my truck. I turned to look at the damage. Bullet holes the size of quarters were spread around the driver's door. He tried to kill me in broad daylight.

"I called the police already. They're on their way," Monica, another one of my coworkers, called from somewhere behind me.

I heard what she said, but I didn't acknowledge her. I was too busy with my thoughts. He actually tried to kill me.

The police got there in record time. Even though I was a victim of a crime and I was kind of reassured they had shown up quickly, I couldn't help but think about why they took so long to get to the hood, but always showed up in the suburbs quickly.

"Are you the victim?" a tall, red-headed detective dressed in a black suit asked.

"Yeah."

"You want to tell me what happened? Did you know the perp?"

"I didn't get a chance to see his face. It happened quick. I was walking to my truck and I noticed a black '90s model Grand Am a few parking spaces over. The windows were tinted, so I couldn't see inside. As soon as the window rolled down and I seen the gun sticking out, I ducked."

"Well, based on the amount of bullets in your truck, we think the gun was automatic. Problem is, there are no shell casings. What kind of gun was it? Are you sure he had it out the window?"

"I'm not really sure if he had it out the window 'cause it all happened fast. But I know the gun was an automatic. Silver."

"So, you remember the silver gun, but you don't remember the shooter?" he asked, looking at me suspiciously.

"Wait. You think I'm lying to you? I just got shot at, man! I was almost killed!" I yelled.

"C'mon, Mr. Swanson. I know guys from your neck of the woods know the drill. Somebody shooting at you a dozen or more times while at work in this fancy accounting firm makes me think it's personal. Help me do my job, Mr. Swanson. Who was the guy and why did he want to kill you?"

All I could do was stare at him. "Get the fuck outta my face, man, and let me talk to a real police officer," I spat.

"You better watch your tone, boy. I will–"

"Detective Richardson, is everything okay?" a female Captain asked as she got in between me and the detective.

"Yeah. Everything is fine, Captain. The victim doesn't know who shot at him or why. I think he's lying," Detective Richardson said, giving me a nasty look.

"Go on over and interview witnesses. I'll handle it from here."

The detective gave me a lingering stare as he walked away.

"Sorry about Richardson. He's a good cop and he means well, but he can be an ass. I'm Captain Taylor. You want to tell me what happened?"

"Someone in a black 90's model Grand Am shot at me. I don't know if it was a man or woman. I didn't get a chance to see their face. The windows were tinted. Whoever it was rolled down the passenger window and started shooting. Once I seen a gun, I ducked for cover."

"Do you have any enemies? Anybody who would want to hurt you?"

"No. I didn't grow up in the streets, and I don't have a beef with anyone."

"Okay, Mr. Swanson. Sit tight. I'll have another officer come and get your statement, and once Crime Scene finishes with your truck, you can go. If you remember anything else, let the officers know."

"Alright, Captain. Thanks."

After talking to two police officers and giving two more statements, I was allowed to leave. I dialed Trigga's number as I drove away.

"Luke. 'Sup, nigga?"

"Pistol tried to kill me," I said flatly.

I could hear disbelief in Trigga's voice. "What?"

"Yeah, man. He tried to kill me."

"What? You a'ight, nigga? When? What happened?"

"About an hour ago. At my job."

"You fuckin' serious? He tried to kill you at work?" Trigga screamed, his voice squeaking.

"Yeah, man. Emptied a clip at me in the parking lot."

"I'm killin' that bitch-ass nigga. Where you at now?"

"On my way home. I gotta drop my truck off at a shop and get a rental car. I can't believe he tried to shoot me."

"Niggas can't take ass-whoopin's now-a-days. Niggas don't fight no more. It's all about raw spelled backward out here. But don't trip, my nigga. I'ma get that bitch!"

"Man. Don't get too deep in this shit, Trigga. I'll find a way to deal with this," I said, wanting to handle this on my own. When Chief was out, he always came to my rescue, and now Trigga was trying to do the same. I didn't want that. But I did have two huge problems: I had never been shot at before, and I didn't even own a gun.

"I told Big Chief I wasn't gon' let shit happen to you, nigga, and I'ma keep my word. I'ma hit chu back later. Answer the phone."

Click.

I tossed my phone on the glass-covered passenger seat and began to think about the shooting. I still couldn't believe Pistol tried to kill me. I didn't know whether to be mad, scared, or sad. I felt a combination of all three. But I mostly felt thankful to be alive.

And then it dawned on me. How did Pistol know where I worked? I felt the anger rising inside of me as I realized my baby mama was complicit in Pistol's attempt on my life. Thoughts of killing them both while they slept flashed in my mind. I wanted to do it. Bad. But thoughts of my brother doing life in prison flashed in my mind. I would also hate to explain to my daughter that her mother was dead. I definitely wasn't looking forward to that. Then there were my parents. If I ended up in jail, it would destroy them.

As I neared Streets Auto Body Shop, I decided to let the streets bury their own. I had too much to lose if I got locked up for murder. But I was going to be taking a precaution. I was buying a gun tomorrow. I wouldn't be caught slipping again.

After dropping my truck off, I called Avis and got a rental vehicle. A black 2013 Dodge Ram. By the time I made it back home, it was almost eight o'clock. I decided to call it a night Even though it was still early and I was supposed to meet with Syn later in the evening. I hit the shower and prepared for bed. I wanted to be alone. I was fried mentally and emotionally. All I wanted to do was sleep.

***

"Hello?"

"Yo, Luke, I need you to come over right away. I need some help."

I looked at the time on my cell phone. "Damn, Trigga. It's past eleven, and I just fell asleep. Can it wait 'til tomorrow?"

"Nah, it can't wait. I really need yo' help with this. Life or death shit. Straight-up."

Trigga sounded way too calm for a life or death emergency.

"Where you at?"

Same house I threw my party at. Remember where it is?"

"Yeah. Let me get dressed. Be there in a few minutes."

After hanging up, I went to my room-closet to find something to wear. I settled on a pair of sweats and Nike Cross Trainers. I didn't know what Trigga's so-called emergency was, but I had a feeling it might need running shoes.

It took me twenty minutes to get to the house Trigga told me to meet him at. I parked the rented Dodge at the curb and climbed the steps to the house. After ringing the doorbell, I waited. It didn't take long for someone to answer.

"Luke. Come in, nigga," Trigga said, giving me a strange look. There was no smile on his face. He wore a serious look.

"What's the emergency?" I asked as I walked past him and into the house.

"Just follow me," he said, his voice matching his facial expression.

The house was dark and empty. It felt a little eerie. I didn't say a word as he led me into the basement. For the first time since I met Trigga, I was kind of scared being with him. I knew whatever he was about to show me was probably something I didn't want to see.

"Here," Trigga mumbled, reaching into the pocket of his dark jeans. He pulled out a big, black revolved.

"What's this for?" I asked, refusing to take the gun.

"See for yo'self," he said, walking toward a closed door at the end of the hall.

When he opened the door, the first things I noticed were the dogs. Two pit bulls. Two of Trigga's boys had them on thick chains. One of the dogs was tan, the other blue. Both of their faces were covered in blood. Fresh blood. I turned my attention to what the dogs were growling at. What I seen almost made me throw up.

"Shit!" I groaned in disbelief.

Pistol was hanging from the ceiling by a chain wrapped around his arms. All he had on was a pair of ripped and bloodied shorts. Chunks of flesh were missing from different parts of his body. I could see the white of bone on his rib cage. His face was swollen and bloody. He looked dead.

"I saved his final breath for you to take," Trigga said, pushing the gun at me again.

"I can't do it, man," I said, closing my eyes and trying to blink away the image of Pistol.

"You sure? This bitch-ass nigga tried to kill you."

"Yeah, I'm sure. I need to leave, man," I said, turning and heading for the stairs.

"I had to keep my word to Big Chief!" Trigga called behind me.

I didn't answer. I stumbled up the stairs and through the house. I had to get out of there. I had never in my life seen anything to gruesome.

Pow!

The single gunshot sopped me in my tracks. It had come from the basement. Pistol was dead. I knew it. And the realization made my lungs feel like they were collapsing. I couldn't breathe!

I ran through the house and out the front door. As soon as the fresh air hit my lungs, I threw up. After heaving guts in the grass, I got into the rental truck and sped away. I kept seeing visions of Pistol in my mind. I couldn't get him out. He was hanging. Bloodied. Half dead. I needed to forget him.

I brought the truck to a screeching stop at the first liquor store I seen. I left the keys in the ignition as I ran inside. I grabbed the first bottle of liquor I saw. Wild Irish Rose. The red kind. I threw a ten dollar bill on the counter and cracked the top. I didn't even care about the change. I turned the bottle upside down and walked out of the store, guzzling the drink like it was water.

When I got back in the truck, I turned the radio up as loud as it would go. I rapped along with Gucci Mane as I sped away.

Some time later, the liquor kicked in and my mind went blank.

I didn't remember driving there, but the next thing I knew, I was at Syncere's club. After I parked, I opened the door to get out and tripped on the step. I fell to the ground and the wine bottle shattered, covering me with glass and liquor. For some reason, I thought it was funny. I laughed loudly as I crawled to by knees, somehow managing to stand. On the walk to the club's entrance, it felt like my legs didn't have muscles or bones. I wobbled and swayed all the way to the door. When I opened it, I stumbled in and fell to the floor. I laughed again.

"Hey, man! What the fuck you doin'?" I heard a man yell as someone lifted me off my feet.

I opened my eyes and seen the biggest, ugliest, builtest, and blackest man I had ever seen. And he was literally holding me in the air.

"Damn, nigga. You ugly as fuck!" I laughed.

"Get the fuck outta here!" he yelled, tossing me like a rag doll.

I bounced off the wall and hit the floor. I knew it was supposed to hurt, but I didn't feel anything.

"Bryce, stop! Luke, what are you doing here?"

I lifted my head and seen Syncere running toward me. I tried to stand, but couldn't. "Syn! Hey, baby. You lookin' good, girl. My fuckin' legs don't work."

"Get up, Luke. What are you doing here, and what have you been drinking?" Syncere asked as she tried to help me stand.

"I need help, Syn," I mumbled as I leaned against her.

"Okay. Come to my office. Tell me what you need me to do."

"I need you to help me forget," I mumbled.

"What are you walking about? Help you forget what?"

"The dead man. Pistol."

"Stop talking, Luke. You're drunk. Lie down."

I felt myself sink onto something cool and soft. I couldn't have gotten up if I wanted to. "I need you to help me forget the dead man, Syn. I need you. I. Gotta. Forget…."

Chapter 18

"Hey, sleepy head," I sang after Luke stirred.

"Hey. Where am I? How did I get here?" he asked, blinking rapidly after opening his eyes.

"You're at my house. You don't remember?"

"No. Don't really remember shit. And my body hurts. My head. My back." He grimaced as he sat up in bed.

"Bryce did that. You came into the club tripping. He roughed you up a little bit, but I stopped him before it got out of hand."

"I'm whoopin' Bryce ass when I catch him," he chuckled.

I pictured him and Bryce fighting. Bryce is ginormous. In my vision, Luke lost. Badly. "Whoa, tiger! Let's not try to fight my staff. I need my guys."

"My mouth is dry. You got something to drink? 7-Up or something?"

"I have just the thing for you," I said as I climbed out of bed. I went to the kitchen and pulled a beer from the fridge.

"Beer?" he questioned, looking at me funny.

"Yeah. I brought this home especially for you. I knew you would need it. And trust me, it works. You should know this remedy from your college days."

"I forgot about this," he said as he took the beer.

I climbed back in the bed and watched him pop the top on the Miller High Life. He drank half in one gulp. I looked him over as he drank. He was shirtless. Luke wasn't a buff guy, but he was in good shape. Fit. Muscles were just right. And looking at his naked torso made me want to rape him.

"Don't think I don't see the way you looking at me," he laughed.

"Guilty," I blushed, pushing him playfully.

"Girl, you betta stop. I ain't drunk no more. Ain't nobody else roughin' me up."

"Whatever. So, what happened last night? What were you talking about?"

"I don't know what you're talking about. What did I say?" he asked, spinning to face me.

"Something about a dead man. Forgetting. Pistol. Isn't that your baby mother's boyfriend?"

I watched Luke's eyes go from clear and bright to dark and cloudy. He remembered, and whatever he remembered, it was bad.

"Luke, tell me what it is."

"Pistol tried to kill me yesterday."

I wasn't expecting him to say that. "Your baby mother's boyfriend? The one you beat up?"

"Yeah. He shot at me when I was leaving work yesterday. Shot up my truck. Guess he couldn't take the ass-whoopin'."

I was beyond shocked. Luke was a nine-to-five guy, not a thug. Accountants and shootouts went together like oil and water. "Oh, my God, Luke! I can't believe he tried to kill you. So, what did you do? You said he was dead. Did you...?"

"Nah. He's dead, but I didn't do it. It was street justice."

I knew not to ask anymore questions. I switched subjects. "So, how is the hangover?"

"It's not that bad. I've had worse. Shit, what time is it?" he asked. His eyes popped as a look of alarm spread across his face.

I grabbed my phone off the bedside table and caught a glance of the clock. Damn, it was later than I'd thought.

"Fuck! Where is my phone? Did I bring my phone?" he asked, looking around the room frantically.

"All you had was your keys. They're in your sweat pants," I said, pointing across the room to the chair his sweat pants sat in.

"I need to call work. Let me see your phone."

I gave it to him and listened as he spoke to someone named Jim about taking the day off.

"So, what do you have planned today?" he asked after giving me back my phone.

"I think I was probably going to laze around all day. Head to the club later."

"Good. That means you can spend the rest of the afternoon in bed helping me forget about yesterday."

"Oh, Luke!" I kissed his lips as he pulled me into his lap. I could taste the beer on his mouth. I wasn't a beer drinker, but I liked the way it tasted coming from his mouth.

As his tongue tangled deliciously with mine, his fingers caressed my booty and his hard chest pressed against my nipples, causing a shockwave of pleasure to run through my body. "Mm," I moaned, rubbing his head, and then I got an idea. "Stop. I got this. Lay back," I said, pulling his head away from my breast.

"Women on top. I like it when a woman is in control," he smiled.

I bent down and began by kissing his neck. I kissed and licked my way down to his chest and started sucking on his nipples. From there I licked my way down his torso, running my tongue across the grooves between his abs. When I got to the V at his waist, I stopped long enough to pull off his boxers. His dick shot into the air like a missile. I admired it for a few moments. It was about eight inches and as thick as a cucumber. The perfect size for me. I wanted to jump on it and ride him 'til I came, but I controlled myself. I had other plans. Plans to make him beg. Like he did me.

I wrapped my fist around the shaft, preparing to take him in my mouth for the first time. I had only given oral sex to two men in my life, but that didn't matter. I knew how to turn a man on. And judging my the way Luke was staring up at me, I definitely turned him on.

I looked him in his eyes as I took his head in my mouth. He closed his eyes for a moment and let out a deep moan. I pumped my hand up and down his length while I sucked him.

When he reached for my head, I stopped. "Hands off," I ordered.

"It's like that, huh?" he smiled as his hands fell to his sides.

I began stroking him with my hand as I moved my face toward his balls. I sucked them, licked them, and kissed them as I stroked him with my hand. When I felt his body tense up, I stopped. I wasn't about to let him get off. Not until he begged. But I made sure to keep him stimulated as I massaged his balls while I placed kisses on his manhood. He reached for my head again. I stopped.

"Don't touch me."

After he dropped his hands at his sides, I began sucking him again, massaging his sack as I took as much of him as I could into my mouth. He started moaning and gripping the bed sheets. Seeing how much pleasure I was bringing him had me so wet I could feel my juices running down my thigh.

When his body began tightening up and he started sucking in deep breaths, I stopped.

"C'mon, Syn. Stop teasing me," he breathed.

"I don't know what you're talking about," I said in between the licks and kisses I was placing up and down the length of him.

"Quit bullshittin', girl."

A Gangsta's Syn

"Say please," I teased.

There was a slight pause. "Please, Syn."

Hearing him say that shit turned me on more than I thought it would. It made me feel powerful. And because he said the magic words, I was about to grant his wish.

I took him in my mouth again and started sucking him hard, swallowing as much of him as I could. It didn't take long for him to cum. He moaned, cursed, and grabbed my hair as I drained him. I didn't care that he was touching me now. My mission had been accomplished.

When I finished sucking him, he was still hard. And I was wet. I jumped on top of him and sat down, sliding him inside me slowly. When he was all the way in, I waited until my walls adjusted for him. And then I rocked his world. I moaned, grunted, and clawed at his chest as I rode him. Fuck cloud nine. I was on cloud ten! And when I came, it was hard. And loud.

"That's all you got?" Luke asked after I fell on top of him. My orgasm had me weak. And he was still inside me. And still hard.

"Wait. I need a minute," I panted.

"No such thing," he said, pushing me off him and rolling me onto my side. He lay on his side as he got behind me.

"Ooh," I moaned, arching my back as he entered me.

He started off slow, then built up a nice and stead long-stroke.

"Oh, shit! Luke! Yes!"

He slammed his pelvis into my backside and I threw it right back t him. It wasn't long before my orgasm was building up again.

This time we came together. And it was good. I was satisfied.

And I think I was falling in love.

Chapter 19

I was sitting at my desk, going over contracts J-Rock had sent me for some of my girls to be in his music videos when my phone rang. I looked down at the number.

"Hello?"

"Syncere?"

I recognized the voice instantly. The smile that spread across my face told of how long I had been waiting to receive this call.

"This is me. Hey, Trinity. I was wondering when you'd call."

"Um, do you have a minute to talk?" She sounded like something was wrong.

I put away the contracts and gave her my undivided attention. "I sure do. What's up?"

"I just got fired from my job."

"What? Really? Why?"

"A.J." She said his name like it left a bad taste in her mouth.

I could feel the anger I harbored for him boil up inside of me. "What did he do?"

"He kept showing up and calling. Harassing me and some of my coworkers. I told him I didn't want to talk to him or see him anymore, but he wouldn't take no for an answer."

I wanted to see her. "So, where are you now?"

"At home. Don't really have much to do. I'm normally at work at this time."

"I knew I should have shot his ass."

"I wish you would've," she laughed.

"Don't tempt me. But forget that fool. How about I come get you and take you to lunch? My treat."

"I can't say no to that."

***

"So, what are you qualified to do?" I asked, staring across the table at Trinity. It felt weird looking at the combination of me and C-Money. She looked like both of us, but mostly him. My nose. The shape and color of my eyes. My hair. The rest was her father. His bushy eyebrows. His thin top lip and big bottom lip. His chin. The shape of his face. Even his pointy ears. As I stared into her brown eyes, admiring our creation, I couldn't help but wonder why she hadn't figured out I was her mother. We didn't look exactly alike, but the resemblance was unmistakable.

"Not much, really. That's why I worked at Foot Locker. I just finished high school. I was taking a little time off before I went to college."

"Where do you plan on going to school?"

"I want to go to Spelman, but I'll probably stay local. Alverno, maybe."

"What will you major?"

"Communication. I think I like the thought of being a radio D.J. or something."

"Sounds good. But in the meantime and in between time, if you want, I could use your help on a business venture. I'm thinking about starting a modeling agency. Ever thought of being a model?" I asked as I lay into my cheese-smothered hash browns.

"What? Me? A model?" she laughed.

I was surprised at how oblivious she was to her beauty. She was dressed down in a pair of jeans, a white t-shirt, and cross trainers, but even in that modest apparel she looked good. There was no denying that.

"Yes, Trinity. A model. You are beautiful. Don't you know that? You can be bigger than all the big-named models. Melissa Ford, Amber Rose, and Tyra Banks ain't got nothing on you, girl!"

"I mean, I know I'm not ugly, but I never thought about being a model."

I liked her humility. It was refreshing. "I believe you can do it. So, what do you say to my offer?" I asked, throwing the opportunity in her lap before she had a chance to talk herself out of it.

"Well, yeah. I guess."

"Good. I will probably have you doing some managerial stuff, too. You'll be a model/manager. Help me get the agency off the ground."

"Wow. Really? I don't know what to say. I have no experience as a manager. You sure you want me?" she asked, doing exactly what I feared she would do. But I wasn't about to let her talk herself out of this one.

"Yes. I'm sure. All you will have to do is smile for the camera, help me find some girls, and fill out some paperwork. Doesn't sound hard, does it?"

"No."

"Good. And what do you have for clothes? What you're your closet look like?"

"What do you mean? Like, high-end stuff?"

"Yes. Dresses, business suits, evening gowns, heels, and bags."

"Um, no. I'm a simple girl. I've always been fine with jeans and t-shirts. And I don't even think I can walk in a pair of heels. I don't see how you do it," she said, glancing down at my red bottoms.

"Well, I'm about to change all of that. Our meal is done. Let's go."

After leaving El Greco's, the first place I drove was to the Prada store. I ended up spending six-thousand dollars in there. Our next step was Macy's. I spent another four-thousand in there. Our last step was Bloomingdales.

"What do you do for a living?" Trinity asked as she stood in the mirror while I adjusted the DeLee dress she was trying on.

"I run a club. Turn this way."

"Really? What's the name of it? Maybe I've heard of it."

Based on how naive she acted, I knew she hadn't heard of my club. "The Den of Syn."

"I like that. The name is creative. But I've never heard of it."

"That's because it's a strip club."

"Really? Like, a naked ladies strip club?" she asked, looking at me through the mirror with wide eyes.

I couldn't stop myself from laughing. "Yes, I employ naked ladies. Sex sells, sweetheart. I make a tidy living."

"I can tell. You've spent more on me in one day than I've spent in the last ten years."

"If you're going to be working with me, then you have to look the part. Plus, have you seen how beautiful you look?"

I stepped back so she could have the mirror to herself. The white form-fitting dress she was trying on showed off her killer curves. All she needed was a trip to the hair salon for a new hairdo and she would be ready for the red carpet.

"I love it, Syncere," she said, striking a few poses.

"This is how you should always feel. There is a diva inside of you, and I will help you bring her out. First thing you gotta do is realize your potential. There is nothing worse than someone seeing more potential in you than you see in yourself. It all starts in the mind. If you don't believe in you, nobody will. The same with beauty. You are beautiful,

Trinity. I mean really, really beautiful. But if you don't think and know it, then your beauty is useless, and your body will reflect how you think. Confidence is a must, also. As a woman, confidence is one of our best assets. It makes us irresistible. And heels are our best friends. A nice pair of shoes can turn a simple outfit into high end fashion."

"Wow, Syncere. You sound like those people on TV. I owe you big time."

"Don't worry about it, baby girl. You are important to me. I will do anything I can to help you."

"So, who are you? Why are you helping me like this?"

I had been thinking of ways to answer questions along this line since the last time I had seen her. I still wasn't comfortable with telling her I was her mom. So, I lied. "We're cousins."

Trinity's eyes lit up. "Really?"

"Yes. Your father was my cousin. His name was Christopher Simmons, A.K.A. C-Money. He was killed a couple months after you were born. By the police. He used to be a big drug dealer, and when he got arrested and found guilty of murder, he snapped. He fought with courtroom bailiffs, took one of their guns, and shot two of them. The police ended up killing him."

Trinity looked like she was about to cry. "Oh, my God! That is horrible."

"I know. But he's in a better place now. You look like him a lot."

"How about my mom? Who is she?"

"Her name is Loretta. I don't know her last name. Only seen her a couple of times."

"Where does she live? Do you know why she left me? And why didn't someone from your family look for me? Why did they let me grow up in group homes and foster care?"

Damn. I knew this would be a hard conversation, but she was making it really hard.

"I haven't seen Loretta since you were little. I don't know why she left you. We weren't that cool. But whatever her reason, I'm sure she had to do it. She loved you, and I know she wouldn't have given you up by choice."

"But what about your side of the family? Why didn't they get me?"

"I don't know. I stopped talking to them when you were a baby. I don't know where any of them live, either. And I'm not really looking forward to seeing them, either."

"Would you help me find them? I have so many questions. I want to know where I came from."

As I stared into the soft brown eyes that looked exactly like mine, I regretted lying to her. I knew I would have to continue the lie because of my cowardice. And I knew whenever the truth came out, it would be ugly. Really ugly. But I couldn't turn back now. Not until we got closer.

"Sure. I'll do whatever I can to help you, but let's get all this stuff up to the counter. I still have a few more things to do before the evening is up."

"Okay. So, how did you find me?" Trinity asked as we headed toward the checkout counter.

"I was talking to a friend awhile back and we started talking about your father. After we reminisced, she asked about you. I told her I didn't know where you were or who you were. Later that kind of sparked my curiosity to find you. I did a search and was led to your door."

"Thanks for looking for me. And thanks for everything. It feels good to know I'm not alone."

Whew.

"I promise I won't ever leave you. I am here, and I have

your back."

***

After dropping Trinity off at home, I headed back to my club. I was only a few blocks away and had just pulled up to a stoplight when my phone rang. I looked at the screen before answering.

"Hey, Luke," I grinned.

"Hey, Super Woman. What you up to?"

"Just finished running some errands. 'Bout to head back to the club. You?"

"Just got off work. Was thinking about coming to see you. Will you be busy all night?"

"Probably not. It's Wednesday. I might leave around midnight, depending on what's happening."

"Want some company?"

"Sure. Why not? I can think of a few things for you to do," I flirted.

"Oh, really? You know, I really like doing things."

"And I like when you do the–"

"Girl, you better stop 'fore you fuck around and not be able to get any work done."

"Don't talk about it. Be about it," I challenged.

"I'm done talking. I gotta run home and change. I'll see you in a few minutes."

I couldn't wipe the smile off my face as I hung up the phone. I never imagined I would have deep feelings for another man. After C-Money died, I became hard. Losing the love of my life had killed a part of me. And spending almost twenty years in prison made it worse. I swore to never fall in love again. Losing loved ones hurt. Not only did I lose the love of my life, but I also lost my parents in a traffic accident, and I lost someone else close to me to the prison system. Those losses had caused me to shut down my heart. But Luke was changing the rules I had set in place.

"Syncere," someone called as soon as I stepped foot in my club.

I looked toward the bar, where the voice had come from. A brown-skinned man wearing a green Adidas cap, a blue t-shirt, belt, blue jeans, and green Adidas shoes got off the bar stool. He looked to be about six feet tall and was skinny. Another man followed behind him. He was taller, about 6'3", was light-skinned, had hair that flowed down his back, and had lots of muscles. He looked Hawaiian. He was dressed in a black t-shirt, gray slacks, and loafers.

"Do I know you?" I asked, looking them both over.

"Nah, not really. But I'm hoping we can change that. Do you have somewhere we can talk?" the skinny man asked, flashing a mouth full of gold teeth.

He didn't look worthy of a chat or my time. He looked like an average street hustler. "Talk about?"

"I have a business arrangement. A proposition, really."

I looked from his mouth to the stern-faced Hawaiian. On the strength of the Hawaiian's serious look, I decided to listen to the business proposition.

"Follow me."

I looked toward Bryce as I led the men back to my office. Bryce nodded his head to let me know he had my back. When I got to my office, the gold-toothed man walked in with me. The other man closed the door behind us and remained outside. I got a funny feeling.

"So, what is this business proposition?" I asked, standing behind my desk and nonchalantly opening my purse as I sat it atop my desk. My gun was inside. I would shoot him if he made a wrong move.

"I have a message from a mutual friend," he said, standing in front of my desk and looking me over.

"Okay. That message is?"

"Mr. Calico says your seven days are up. I can't leave here without yo' name on a contract."

"Tell Mr. Calico my answer is no. I don't have his money. Now, I have business to attend to. Could you please leave?"

"See, I don't think you understand me, Syncere. You have no choice. Yo' time is up. Dis a collection call."

"Fuck you and Calico."

I reached for my purse, but Calico's henchman was faster. He pulled out a big, black automatic handgun.

"Getcho muthafuckin' hand out dat purse," he demanded, pointing the gun at me.

While I did what I was told, he grabbed my purse.

"Oh, shit! Bitch tried to shoot a nigga, huh?" he laughed, pulling out my gun. "You gon' pay for that shit, bitch. But for now, sign this," he said, pull an envelope from his pocket.

"What is–" I was saying when I heard voices outside my door. Bryce! He and the Hawaiian were having words. I heard a thud as someone or something hit the floor. A smile spread across my face. "My bodyguard is about to come in here. You should really leave now," I taunted the skinny thug. He had the gun, but the power had just shifted heavily in my favor.

To my surprise, the street punk didn't budge. No fear showed in his eyes. He was actually smiling and still pointing the gun at me. Then my office door opened up. The Hawaiian walked in carrying Bryce in his arms. He was out cold.

After dropping Bryce on the floor, he turned and left. For

the first time in a long time, I got scared.

"Open the envelope and sign the contract, bitch!"

Chapter 20

I had a lot of things in store for Syn tonight. Hearing the way she challenged me over the phone forced me to abandon my plans to go home and shower. After hanging up the phone, I drove straight over to her club. My plan was to get an office quickie, give it to her rough for how she talked to me over the phone, then later tonight I would make her beg me to make her cum.

Teasing and edging each other to the brink of ecstasy had become a regular thing when we had sex. I liked to think of it as plays for power, both of us trying to gain total domination over the other. It was just as erotic as it was fun, and tonight I planned on laying my claim to the majority of the power.

I pulled into the parking lot of The Den of Syn and parked my freshly-repaired truck next to Syn's sports car. I was pleased when I walked inside and found the early evening crowd to be sparse. Good. That meant I could have Syn to myself for a little while and no one would miss her.

After speaking to a few of the girls on the floor, I made my way to the bar. Jayda was tending. Jayda was a sexy black creation with a short silver afro, nice lips, and a tight body. She always gave me sexy smiles and long stares.

"'Sup, Jayda? Where is Syn?" I asked, slapping my hands on the bar top.

"Hey, Luke," she smiled, giving me 'the look.' "Syn is in the office. She's having a meeting or something. Been awhile. Bryce went back there a few minutes ago."

"Okay. Guess I should give her a few minutes. Uh, let me get a beer. That black label," I said, having a seat on a stool.

"Gotcha," she said before turning and switching toward

the coolers. I couldn't help but watch her ass in the tight, black leather pants. It was muscular. Looked like she could crack walnuts with her cheeks.

"Here you go. It's on the house," she said after popping the top and sliding over the sixteen ounce bottle.

"Thanks," I said before taking a long drink.

"What have you been doing to my girl, Luke? Around you, I see a side of her I have never seen," Jayda said, resting her elbows on the bar and looking at me like I knew magic.

"Do you believe in destiny, Jayda?"

"I don't know. When I was in my twenties, yes. But now that I am almost forty, I am second guessing it."

"You know, the beautiful thing about destiny is we can choose our own. Our destiny isn't tied to one person or one thing. We can have several destinies."

"And so, you're saying…?"

"That Syn is experiencing destiny," I smiled.

"You are way too cocky," she laughed, shaking her head in disbelief.

"The truth can't be cocky. The truth is the truth. If she is not experiencing destiny, then what do you call it?" I asked, taking a sip of my beer.

"Good dick," she answered bluntly.

I almost spit my beer all over the bar as I burst out laughing. "And that, too," I agreed in between laughter.

I sat and talked with Jayda for a few more minutes before deciding to crash Syn's meeting. I just wanted to peek my head in and let her know I was here. I sipped my beer as I walked down the hall toward her office. I noticed a big thug-looking brother standing outside her door like he was a solider on post. I had seen Syn's security staff, and I didn't remember seeing him. I figured he was new.

"Hey, man. Could you tell Syn that Luke is here?" I

asked as I neared him.

"She busy," he said flatly.

"Yeah, I heard. But she's expecting me."

"I said she busy, nigga. Get the fuck outta here!"

His words surprised me. I was at a loss for words. I wanted to hit him in the mouth, but as I looked him over, I thought better. He out-weighed me by about thirty pounds and a lot of muscle. One thing that went in my favor was we were about the same height.

So, instead of swinging a fist at him, I snapped, "Who the fuck you talkin' to like that? Do you work for Syn? 'Cause if you do and you want to keep your job, then you need to move yo' ass outta my way!"

His muscles twitched, and I seen the punch coming before he threw it. I tried to dodge it, but the big man was fast. Really fast. His knuckles grazed my chin. Had I taken the full brunt of the blow, he would've knocked me out.

I stumbled backward, trying to keep my footing. I looked up just in time to see him coming at me, swinging a flurry of punches. I dodged them all. When he seen I could fight, he stopped and got into a boxer's stance. I did, too, keeping the beer bottle in my band. I knew I would probably need it as a weapon.

But before I got the chance to go on the offensive, he rushed me. He swung punches and kicks like he was Bruce Lee. This motherfucker knew karate!

I dodged punch after punch and kick after kick. I did so much running and ducking that we went down the hall and ended up in the middle of the club. I could hear gasps, women scream, and furniture flying. But I never took my eyes off Jackie Chan.

When he finished his offensive onslaught, I broke the bottle and threw a few punches. He dodged my attack.

Easily.

We squared up again. I still had the bottle at the ready. He crept toward me, closing in for the kill. I eased back slowly, keeping a few feet in between us. I figured my only chance to beat him would be by throwing the bottle and making him flinch. Then I would have to use the distraction to get in a couple punches.

We must've been thinking about attacking each other at the same time, because as soon as I cocked the bottle back, he launched a kick. His foot landed in my stomach as the bottle flew from my hand. I stumbled backward, trying to keep my balance. I ended up running into a table and falling to the floor.

When I looked up, he was on his knees, grabbing his face. Blood was gushing between his fingers. The bottle had landed a direct hit. I looked for something else to hit him with. Seeing a medium-sized crystal ashtray on a table near me, I got up and grabbed it. When I spun toward the karate kid, he was reaching one of his bloody hands down to his waist. I threw the ashtray like I was throwing a football. He roared when the hard crystal connected with his face, dropping the gun he pulled from his waist.

I seized the opportunity to put him out of his misery. I ran at him with my fist cocked back. I could feel his jaw break when my fist connected with his chin. He fell to the floor like a downed tree. He was out.

I reached for the black gun lying next to him, and that's when I noticed the silencer. I knew the man I had just knocked out and whoever was in Syn's office were here on serious business, and Syn could be in trouble.

With gun in hand, I ran down the hall and burst into Syn's office like I was the SWAT Team. What happened when I entered that room only took a second or two, but it

162

seemed like it lasted hours.

The first thing I noticed was Bryce lying on the floor in an unconscious heap of muscles.

I looked across the room and seen a man and Syncere locked in a wrestling match. He was winning. He had his hands wrapped around her throat, choking her.

Her face was bloody and tears were mixing with her blood.

The man looked startled when he seen me. Then he went for his waist.

I raised the silenced pistol and kept shooting until he fell on the ground.

"Luke!" Syncere screamed, running toward me. She slammed into me and hugged me.

I didn't even feel her touch me. My body had gone numb.

"I'm so happy to see you, baby," she cried.

"Is he dead? I shot him. Is he dead?" I asked when I got my voice back. I felt panicked.

"Calm down, Luke."

"I shot him! We have to help him! Call an ambulance!" I yelled, pushing her away as I walked toward her desk to check on him. When I laid eyes on him, I almost had a heart attack. "Oh, shit! Oh, shit! He's dying!"

The man was sprawled out on the floor behind her desk, choking on his own blood. There were several bullet holes in his chest and neck. I didn't know how many times I fired the gun, but it didn't look like I missed one shot.

"Get away from him!" I heard Syncere scream.

I ignored her and bent down beside him. I wanted to try to stop the bleeding. Problem was, he had so much blood coming out of him that I didn't know where to start.

And then he stopped choking. Or moving. Or breathing.

"Call the police!" I screamed as the panic fully set in.

"No, Luke. Not yet," Syn yelled, pulling me away from the body.

"Is everything okay?" Jayda asked, appearing in the door. She couldn't see the body because it was behind the desk, but she did see Bryce on the floor and the gun in my hand.

"Jayda, call an ambulance! Hurry up!" I screamed.

"No, Jayda. Wait!" Syn yelled.

"Syn, he's dead. We gotta call the police," I said, pulling out my phone.

"No, Luke!" she screamed. Before I could dial 911, she ran over and snatched my phone from me. "No police. I'll handle this. Jayda, where is the other one?"

"He got up and ran out of the club after Luke beat him up. Is everything okay?" she asked, trying to sneak a peek behind the desk.

"I'll explain it all later. Make sure nobody comes down this hall. Close up and keep the girls calm," Syn said as she pushed Jayda out of the office and closed the door.

"Syn, we gotta tell them it was self-defense. I can't go to jail for this shit. He was about to shoot me. He was choking you. The other–"

"Luke!" Syn screamed my name, stopping me from talking. "Calm down and trust me. We're not calling anybody. We have to get rid of the body."

I looked at her like she had talked about my mother. "What? No, we gotta tell them it was self-defense. I need to get my side of the story out."

"Luke. Stop. We're not calling the police. We don't have to tell them anything if they don't find a body."

I stopped to think about what she had just said. She had a point. But what if the police did find him? Then what? I had never been in trouble with the police before, and I wanted to do the right thing. "I don't know about this," I mumbled.

"Trust me," she said before going over to wake up Bryce. After a few slaps to the face, he opened his eyes.

"Shit. What the fuck happened?" he asked, struggling to get to his feet.

"Luke shot one of those dudes. I need your help."

Bryce grabbed his jaw and shook his head. "A'ight. But where that Hawaiian-looking motherfucker at? I want my revenge."

"He's gone. But the other one is behind my desk."

I eyed Bryce as he went to look behind Syn's desk. This dude was huge and looked like a body builder. It surprised me that he got knocked out.

"Damn. You did this shit, Luke?" he asked, spinning to face me.

"I didn't have a choice, man. He would've killed me."

Bryce wore the smile of a proud father. "My nigga, that's what his bitch-ass get. I owe you one."

"We have to wrap him up. Use this rug. Luke, can you bring your truck around back? We have to get him out of here," Syn said as she dragged the sizable rug over to the body.

"What? Hell no! I ain't ridin' around with a dead body in the back of my truck," I snapped. I couldn't believe she even asked me something like that.

"Luke, aye, man, you don't have a choice. Gotta roll with the boss lady on this one," Bryce said as he wrapped the bloody body in the rug.

"Trust me, Luke. We have to make him disappear," Syn said, walking over to me and searching my face.

I stared down into her eyes. They were different. Hard. And clear. And her demeanor was calm. It surprised me. I didn't understand why her and Bryce weren't panicking, or at least showing signs of being nervous.

"Okay," I reluctantly agreed.

It seemed like they knew what they were doing, so I had to trust them. I turned and headed for the door.

"Luke!" Syn called after me.

I spun around. "Yeah."

"Put up the gun."

I looked down and seen the gun still in my fist. "Shit."

After waisting the gun, I left the office. All eyes were on me as I walked through the club. Most of the patrons had left, but there were a few stragglers and a couple of dancers hanging around. I didn't look any of them in the eyes. It felt like they all knew I had killed someone. I began to wonder if they heard the gunshots. Then I remembered the gun had a silencer. I didn't even remember hearing the gun go off because of the thundering of my heart.

Thankfully, I made it out into the parking lot without anyone approaching me. When I got into my truck. I thought about bailing on Syn and Bryce. But I knew I couldn't leave them. Not only were they witnesses, but I liked Syn. So I pulled the truck around back and waited.

"Where we going?" I asked Syn after Bryce loaded the body in the capped flatbed of my truck.

"To Dodge County. Outskirts of Beaver Dam."

I looked over at her like she had just told me the mother ship was coming. "What? You want me to drive the highway with a dead body?"

"Yes. I have a friend. She owns a pig farm. We have to make him disappear."

"Shit. Syn, that's an hour away."

"Do the speed limit."

She was way too calm for me. Like she had done all of

166

this before. "Who the hell are you? And who is this man in my flat-bed?"

"You know me, Luke. I'm tryin' to help you. And I don't know who he was. First time I ever seen him."

"Why was he in your club? Why was he choking you? Who was the other guy?"

"I told you, I don't know. I've never seen them before today. The less you know, the better. Now, will you drive?"

"Fuck that, Syn! My ass is on the line. I killed him. Stop keepin' secrets from me. Tell me what you know."

She looked over at me with cold eyes. Her light brown eyes had gone a shade darker. I was now talking to her alter ego. "I'm sayin' don't ask me anymore. Just drive."

I wanted to argue with her, but the coldness in her voice and look in her eyes told me her words were final. This wasn't the Syn I had bonded with mentally and sexually. She wore a game face, poker face, and stone face all in one.

As I drove away from the club, careful to obey all traffic laws, I began to wonder if her initial rejection of me and her playing hard-to-get was for my benefit. For my protection. I couldn't help but wonder if I had damned my own self by refusing to take no for an answer. It felt like I had been literally tempted by sin.

We didn't say a word as I drove. Hundreds of questions ran through my mind, and I didn't have answers for any of them. But I knew one thing for sure. After we got rid of this body, I would definitely have to evaluate the dynamics of our relationship.

Chapter 21

"So, when did they say your apartment will he ready? Because I'm tired of my woman neglecting me and treating you like you her man," my father grumbled, eyeing me from across the kitchen table.

"Couple days, I guess. The building is being fumigated, Pop. You know they use that high-powered stuff nowadays," I managed in between bites of my cheese eggs. I was hoping to enjoy my blueberry waffles, cheese eggs, and sausage patties, but it looked like Pop had other pans. And wanting to argue was one of them.

"Well, I sure can't wait for you to be gone. I love you, don, but it can only be on man 'living' in this house. When you was a boy, it was fine. But you ain't a boy now. Got cho own place. You need to be sleeping there."

"C'mon, Dad. It ain't that bad. Stop exaggerating. It's only been a week."

"Yeah. A week too long."

"Baby, you can stay as long as you want. Your father is just mad because I can't spoil him," my mother chimed in from over by the stove.

"Damn right! It's only one king in this castle," Pop yelled, slapping his hand on the table for effect.

"Pop, chill. I'm about to leave for work. Have mom 'spoil' you while I'm gone," I said, sipping my cran-apple juice as I got up from the table. He had spoiled my appetite.

"Don't worry 'bout my spoiling. I got all the spoiling I want, whether you here or not."

"Too much info, Dad," I said as I walked over to kiss Mom.

"If you was at home, you wouldn't have to hear it!" Pop called after me.

I didn't respond. I left the house, letting him have the last word. I hated having to stay with my parents. Hated it just as much as Pop hated having me there. I missed my couches, bed, shower, room, closet. Shoot, I missed my whole apartment.

Problem was, I didn't feel safe going home. I didn't want to be in a house alone. I had a hard time sleeping, and when I was able to get to sleep, I was tormented by nightmares of Pistol and the man from Syn's club. In my nightmares, they never died. Sometimes they killed me. I always woke up drenched in sweat, and I never went back to sleep.

Another reason I didn't want to go home was Syncere. She knew where I lived. For the entire week I had been camping out at my parents', I had been avoiding her. I never answered her calls, and I deleted all of her messages. I knew I would probably have to face her sooner or later, and I was hoping it would be later. Way later.

There were still too many questions I didn't have answers to. I still didn't know who I killed or why they were trying to kill her. Or if they were out looking for me now. Syn's past was mysterious, and the fact she didn't want to dig into it made it worse.

And then there was this calmness on her face after the murder that surprised me. She acted like she had done it before. Like she had killed. And if she had, could I be next on that list if I hurt her? I remembered her looking into her purse the night I met her at Joey's when Big Mo was harassing her. I knew there was a gun in that purse, and I knew for certain if I hadn't intervened, she would have clapped that nigga without hesitation.

So, for now, I was keeping away from her.

After leaving my parents', I hopped in my truck and began my trek to work. Work was interesting, to say the least. Ever since I had been shot at, things had been different. My coworkers whispered about me. Some of them were scared to be around me, and the bosses had even hired an armed security guard. To say it was tense around the office was an understatement, but I planned to weather the storm. Pistol was dead, so I didn't have to worry about revenge. Plus, working at Marty and Sloans was exclusive. I made almost six figures a year. No way was I walking away from that.

I was driving and rapping along to J-Cole when my phone began to vibrate. I pulled it from the inside pocket of my navy blue jacket and checked the screen. I couldn't stop myself from smiling as I answered.

"Hey, baby girl. You woke kinda early, ain't you?"

"Hey, Daddy. I wanted to catch you before you went to work."

"I'm on my way now. What's so important?"

"Daddy, can you drop me off some money before you go in? I wanna go to the circus today, and Mommy don't got no money."

I checked my Bulova watch. It was three minutes to seven. I had to be to work by eight. My dad's grumbling had forced me to leave early, and now I had a few minute to spare.

"Okay. I'll be over there in a few minutes."

I made a detour from my work route and pulled up to Shay's house ten minutes later. A chill ran through my body as I parked behind Pistol's SUV. Every time I seen the suburban, I got goosebumps and his dead face flashed in my mind. I was hoping Shay would eventually sell it. I hated looking at it.

After cutting my ignition and pushing thought of Pistol from my mind, I climbed from my truck. I walked up on the porch, and before I had a chance to ring the doorbell, the door opened.

"Hey, Luke. Come in," Shay smiled, looking cheery.

Her demeanor surprised me. I had seen her a few times since Pistol died, and this was the best she had looked. Just a few days ago she looked distraught and angry, but today she was good. She looked stress-free and at peace. The green bathrobe was hugging her in all the right places.

"Hey, Shay. Where is Latia? I need to drop her some money before I go to work."

"She's up in her room. When you come back down, can we talk for a few minutes before you leave?"

I searched her face for a sign of what she wanted to talk to me about. I never told her about Pistol shooting at me, and I never confronted her about how he found out where I worked. He was dead, so I decided to let it go. But now that she wanted to talk, I was beginning to wonder if she had found out anything.

"Uh, yeah. Sure," I agreed before going up to give Latia the money.

When I came back downstairs, I searched the house for Shay. I found her in her room. She was sitting on her bed, doing her hair. I didn't want to go in the room, so I stood in the doorway. "What did you want to talk to me about?"

"Boy, get on in here. You ain't gotta act like that. You use to love me. Remember?" she asked, staring at my reflection in the mirror.

I didn't acknowledge her comment about me loving her once upon a time, but I did step further into the room. "Look, I gotta be to work by eight. What's up?" I didn't like being around Shay any longer than I had to. I didn't hate her, but she was not one of my favorite people.

"Pistol is dead," she said flatly, staring through the

mirror with sad eyes.

"W-what? How-how do you know?" I stuttered, hoping I acted as surprised as I was trying to look.

"I can feel it in my heart. It's been a couple of weeks now. I finally accepted it yesterday. They still haven't found his body, but I know."

"Damn, Shay. I don't know what to say." And I didn't. I didn't want to encourage her to keep hope alive when I knew he was gone.

"You don't have to say anything. I know you didn't like him. He didn't like you, either."

That was an understatement. "So, what did you want to talk to me about? Pistol?" I asked, hoping she hadn't stalled me to be a shoulder she could cry on. It wasn't that kind of party.

"No. I wanted to talk to you about us. I want us to be a family again," she said, getting up from the bed and walking toward me.

If the look on her face wasn't so serious, I would have laughed. I couldn't believe she wanted to talk to me about 'us'. "Us? Shay, you cheated on me a couple of times. I can't trust you." I wanted to mention her telling Pistol where I worked, but I figured her cheating ways would be enough.

"I know what I did was wrong, Luke. And I'm sorry. I really am. I was young and confused. But we're older now. Wiser. And better."

"You're just hurting right now. You think you want me, but you don't. I can't do this." I turned to leave, but she grabbed my arm.

"What about just spending some time with me and Latia? Please, Luke."

"I don't think we should do that, Shay."

"Just one time. I promise, if it don't feel right, then I

won't ask you again. But I just want Latia to see us together for a change. Show her we are done fighting and we can get along."

I wanted to scream *hell no* and leave, but the mentioning of Latia made me think about what Shay was saying. And she had a point. It wasn't a good point, but it was a point nonetheless. It would be good for my daughter to see me and her mom functioning cordially. She had told me on several occasions it saddened her when me and her mother fought.

"Okay. Just once," I gave in.

A smile spread across her face like she won the lotto. "Thanks, Luke. Will you come over after work? We can go to the circus together."

"A'ight. We can do that."

"Can I have a hug?" she asked, opening her arms and giving me a sheepish look.

"Sure."

I opened my arms to receive her, and we hugged for a few moments. I would have never thought the death of Pistol would bring us closer, but it did. When I opened my arms to release her, she didn't let go. Instead, she reached up and kissed me.

I was surprised. I didn't expect it to happen, and even though she wasn't one of my favorite people, I had to admit her lips felt good. It had been a week since I had sex, so when Shay's tongue parted my lips, I didn't stop her. I had known her mouth so well, plus her body pressing into mine felt damned good.

My baby mama wasn't all that fine, maybe a seven on a scale of one through ten, but her body was flawless. Double-Ds on top, small waist, and an ass big enough to have a picnic on.

I used my foot to kick the door closed before we fell onto

the bed. She straddled me and started grinding on me as we kissed. Givenchy got harder than an anvil. I snatched the belt on her robe loose and rolled on top of her. I opened her robe, preparing to put my lips on her double-D's, when I seen it above her left breast. It turned me off instantly, like I had been splashed with cold water.

"What? Why you stop?" she asked, searching my face with wide and horny eyes.

"When you get that?" I asked, looking at the tattoo like it was poison ivy. Pistol's name was drawn on the inside of a heart.

"I had it for a couple of months. Why you trippin'?"

"I gotta get to work," I said, getting up from the bed. Seeing that tat made something click in my mind. She was going to let Pistol kill me. No way was I fucking her. I don't know what I had been thinking.

"Wait. Luke!" She grabbed at me.

I snatched away from her. "Let me go!"

"What the fuck, Luke? You gay now, nigga?" she called after me.

I didn't answer her. I was trying to get out of that house as fast as I could. I didn't know what I had been thinking.

"Pistol was right about you. You is a bitch-ass nigga."

I was halfway down the hall when she said it, but I heard her loud and clear like she was standing next to me. I spun on my heels and walked back to her room. She didn't have a chance to move before my hand was wrapped around her throat. I pushed her up against the wall and started squeezing.

"I know yo' punk-ass told Pistol where I work at. That's why that bitch-ass nigga dead. Keep fuckin' wit' me and I'ma bury yo' ass next to him," I whispered in her ear before dropping her onto the floor and leaving.

***

I couldn't get into my work. I had been sitting at my desk for two hours and hadn't done a thing. I kept thinking about choking Shay and what I had said to her. In that moment, I wanted to kill her. I had to force myself to stop choking her. Watching her eyes bulge and seeing her gasp for air had excited me. I had never felt like that before. I had never wanted to kill someone so badly. And as I sat and thought about wanting to kill her, it scared me. I had already killed someone, and now I wanted to kill again. It made me wonder if I was changing. Becoming like my brother.

"Mr. Swanson?" the intercom on my desk phone chirped. It was one of the secretaries.

"Yeah."

"There is a woman here to see you. Syncere Evans. She says you're expecting her."

Fuck! I wasn't ready to deal with her now, but she was here. She had popped up unannounced. And if I didn't see her. I would look like the biggest coward on the planet.

"Um. S-send her in," I stuttered.

When the intercom clicked off, my heart began to race and my pits began to perspire. It didn't feel normal. I felt like I was having a stroke or something. I got the chills and my mouth became as dry as a desert. I grabbed the bottle of water off my desk and chugged it.

I had just finished quenching my thirst when my office door opened. There was Syn, all 5'7" of her.

"Um, hey. Come in," I mumbled as I stood.

She strode into my office like she meant business, slamming the door behind her. Her hair was pulled into a ponytail and she wore a knee-length yellow dress that hugged her in all the right places. But I couldn't focus on her curves. I was too busy staring into her eyes. They were on fire. She was mad.

Shit!

"We don't have to play kiddie games, Luke. We're not in middle school. If you don't want to talk to me, you should've told me."

"Listen, Syn, It's not like that. It's–"

"What is it like, Luke? Did you read a book in college that can explain this? You got a theory you can use to explain why you haven't called me back? Got another spiel about destiny you can quote to help me see why you haven't been home?"

I tried to think of a response. I stared into her angry eyes and thought as hard as I could. Nothing came. I was drawing blanks. For the first time since I met her, I didn't have a slick comeback. I was speechless. Couldn't say jack shit. So, what I said next sounded something like this:

"I'm sorry, Syn."

She looked at me like I had slapped her.

"Sorry? Sorry? That's all you have to say, Mr. My-Daddy-Taught-Me-To-Be-Chivalrous? Mr. I'm-A-Real-Man? You mean all you have to say is 'sorry?'" she yelled.

"Syn, you gotta calm down. This is my job."

"Fuck that, Luke! This is my life. You told me all that shit and got me to trust you. I let my walls down and let you in. I sucked yo' dick! I don't just go around suckin' dick. I trusted you, and you turned around and left me like I was some ho. I'm not a ho, Luke!"

"I know, Syn. I didn't say you were. But you gotta calm down," I said as I walked over to lock the door.

"I'm pissed off, Luke. You played me."

"I didn't play you. I swear. I just needed some time to

think."

She calmed down. A little. "Why didn't you tell me that? I would have understood."

"I don't know. A lot of shit has happened in the last couple of weeks. Shit that is changing me. Shit I don't understand."

"But that doesn't mean you shut me out. That doesn't mean you leave me out in the cold. I thought we had something, but now I see we don't. I see you can't trust me like I trust you."

"We, do have something, Syn. I can't define it, but I know we have it. It's just. You're secretive. You have different sides. I thought I knew you, but now I feel like I don't."

"You do know me, Luke. You know a side of me no one knows. I gave that to you because I thought you were special. But there is more to me. A lot more. And I know I haven't told you everything, but I can't. Not right now."

"So who doesn't trust who?"

"Okay. I accept that. I haven't been totally honest, but I have my reasons. You just have to give me time. I'm not the kind of girl that just opens up like that. I have been through a lot. I've been hurt and betrayed by people close to me."

"And so have I, Syn. I know what that feels like, and I didn't mean to do that to you. I just needed time to think."

She paused and gave me a suspicious look. "So, have you thought?"

"Yeah."

"And?"

I hesitated, wondering if I should reveal everything I had been thinking and feeling.

Syn just stared up at me. Waiting.

"The day I killed that man in your club, I seen a side of

you that scared me. Not scared me as if I'm frightened of you, but scared in the sense I know you can get me into trouble. You're involved in some deep shit. And because I'm involved with you, I got into it. And now I have blood on my hands. I don't want blood on my hands."

"I understand how you feel, Luke. I never meant to get you into any trouble. I didn't know they would show up at my club. And I didn't know you would kill someone. But you saved me. I know you always call me your Super Woman, but that day you were my Superman."

Damn. That was a good line. Actually made me feel justified in killing the guy.

"I just have to know one thing, Syn. To ease my conscience."

"Okay."

"Who were they? I'm being tormented by him at night, and I have to know why he was in the club."

"They tried to rob me."

She said it flatly. There was no conviction in her voice or on her face. She had also answered too quickly. Like she had rehearsed her answer. I knew she had lied to me. She still wasn't ready to open up to me. Either that or she still didn't trust me.

"Okay." I decided her explanation was enough. For now.

"So, what now?" she asked, searching my face. It felt like we were back in the restaurant's parking lot all over again. She wanted me to make the next move.

"I guess we do what feels right."

"Can you handle a woman like me?" she asked, staring at me intently. She was looking past my exterior and deep into me, feeling me out. Assessing me.

"What kind of question is that?" I didn't like her questioning if I could handle her. I had killed someone because of her, and now she was questioning me?

"I mean, I have layers. Like an onion. Can you handle me? Or are you one of those fair weather guys? Only stay around when the skies are sunny and clear."

I thought about what she was really saying. In a roundabout way, she was asking me if I would leave her again if shit hit the fan. "I can handle you, Syn. All of you."

Her face was serious, but I seen a smile in her eyes. My Syn was back.

"Show me," she challenged.

Sparks exploded all over my body when our lips met. I had missed the feel of her. My body yearned for her essence. How she felt. How she smelled. The sounds of her moans. I was addicted to Syn. I didn't know where my path with her would lead, but I wanted to travel it.

When I threw her onto my desk, I could hear things fall to the floor, but I didn't care. I needed to be inside of her. I had never had office sex before, but we were about to change that.

She tugged at my belt buckle as I spread her legs. I reached under her dress to pull her panties off only to discover she wasn't wearing any. Damn! She had planned this. She knew she would get her man.

We continued to kiss and moan as she undid my pants. When she freed me from my boxers and pulled me into her flesh, it felt like every nerve ending in my body was being stimulated. She was hot, tight, and wet. I dove deep into her with slow, long strokes. She moaned in my ear, sucked my neck, and bit me.

It didn't take me long to get my rocks off. And when I busted my nut, it tickled my brain.

Chapter 22

"*You got it. You got it bad. When you're on the phone, hang up, and you call right back. Ooh, you got it. You got it bad. When you miss a day without your friend, your whole life's off track*," Luke sang, tearing up the Usher track.

We were riding in his truck, listening to the local radio station. We had just come back from eating and had been talking. When the song came on, he turned up the radio and began singing along.

"Okay, Luke. Stop! Usher is going to sue your ass," I laughed.

He ignored me and kept snapping his finger and singing. "*Said I'm fortunate to have you girl. I want you to know I really adore you. And all my people know what's going on. Look at your mate. Help me sing my song.*"

"I used to like this song. Damn. You're wrong," I laughed, leaning against the door and watching him fail his audition for amateur night.

"Man, that was my jam," he smiled, turning down the radio when the song went off.

"Used to be my song, too. 'Til you started singing it. And it sounds like you still got it bad, too," I cracked, doing a little bit of fishing for information.

When we made up a couple days ago, he said he couldn't put what we had into words. I was hoping the Usher song had helped him. We still hadn't talked about us being in a relationship, but I knew we were more than friends.

"What? Nah, you the one got it bad. Can't go a day without gettin' you some Luke," he laughed,

"Shut up!" I pushed him. There was some truth to what he said, though. I wanted him every day and every night. "Don't act like you don't got it bad, either. '*Ooh, Syn!*

Please make me nut,'" I mocked him.

"Oh, shit! I know you ain't talkin'. *'Please, Luke. Please make me cum. I've never felt so good in my life!'"* he mocked me, adding some embellishments.

"Stop playing! I didn't say all that," I laughed, pushing him again.

"C'mon, Syncere. You know you whipped on my shit."

"You know what, Luke? I'm–" I was saying when my phone began to vibrate. "Wait. Let me get this. Hello?"

"Syncere, can you come over? I need your help," Trinity whispered.

When I heard the fear in <u>her </u>voice, my playful mood left and I shot up in my seat. "Trinity, what's wrong?"

"A.J. is here. He's trying to fight me. I need your help."

"Where are you?"

"I'm at home. In the bathroom."

"Okay. I'm on my way."

"What is it?" Luke asked after I hung up.

"I have to go help my little cousin. Her boyfriend is beating her up."

"Where is she?"

"Over on the south side."

During the ride over to Trinity's house, I rocked in my seat and bit my lips. I kept fearing the worst. What if he hurt her? What if I never got the chance to tell her who I was? Why didn't I shoot his ass the first time? These thoughts bombarded me, and I couldn't stop them from roaming through my mind.

When we got to her house, I got the shock of my life when Luke opened up his glove box and pulled out a black handgun. "When did you get that?"

"Right after Pistol shot at me. Last time I get caught slippin'," he said as he checked to make sure the gun was loaded.

When we walked up on the porch, I put my ear to the door and listened for voices. I didn't hear anything, so I tried the knob. It was unlocked. I gave Luke a look as I opened it. He nodded and followed behind me.

The living room was empty. We crept toward the hall, and that's when I heard voices.

"I told you, you ain't gon' neva leave me. You mine. You gon' always be mine," A.J. said.

I wished I would have shot his ass.

"Get off me. You're hurting my arm!" Trinity whined.

"I don't give a fuck. You my bitch. I own you."

As we continued to creep down the hall, I discovered their voices were coming from the bedroom at the end of the hall. When we were outside the door, I peeked in. They were on the bed. Trinity was lying on her back. A.J. was on top of her, pinning her down.

"So, you like to hit girls, huh?" I asked as Luke and I stepped into the room.

A.J. looked startled as he jumped off the bed. When he seen me and Luke, his eyes got wide as a crack addict's. He began looking around the room like he was trying to find a way out.

"I got this, Syn," Luke stepped forward. "My pop told me about cowards like him. They like to hit girls, but can't hit a man."

I really wanted to see how this would end. When Luke told me about him beating up the big Hawaiian who knocked out Bryce, it excited me. I wanted to see him in action.

"I ain't no coward, nigga," A.J. said in a shaky voice.

Luke stepped further into the room, stopping when him a and A.J. were a few feet apart. "Well, show me. Show me you ain't a bitch-ass nigga. Show me my daddy was wrong.

Show me you can fight a man, pussy."

A.J. hesitated before he swung. His punch was so slow I could have dodged it.

"Now, if that was yo' best shot, then my daddy was right. You is a bitch. And you can't fight," Luke taunted him after dodging the slow-motion punch.

I could see the anger flash in A.J.'s eyes. He swung again. Luke dodged it and slapped him so hard that I felt it.

"I can't believe you let him hit you, Trinity. He's a bitch," Luke laughed.

A.J. must've been really fed up with Luke, because he ran at him, swinging wild punches. Luke side-stepped him and threw one of the fastest punches I had ever seen. It landed right on A.J.'s jaw. He fell on the floor and stayed there.

I was impressed and turned on. "Damn, Luke!"

"Thank y'all for coming, Syncere," Trinity said, getting off the bed and coming to hug me.

"I told you I have your back."

"I'ma take him outside," Luke said, grabbing A.J. by the foot and dragging him out of the room. When he was gone, I turned to Trinity.

"What was he doing over here? How did he get in?" I knew she had let him in, and I was angry.

"I let him in. He kept begging me. I got tired of say no," she said weakly.

I decided not to lecture her. A.J. had hit her, and she was probably beating herself up on the inside.

"Well, hopefully you've learned your lesson. I told you his ass was no good. I don't care how much he begs, don't let his ass back in your house," I said sternly.

"I won't. I promise. I don't got time for his shit."

"Good. Do you want to stay with me for a couple of

days?" I asked. I wanted to keep an eye on her and teach her a few things.

"Can I?"

"Sure. Grab what you need. I'm going to check on Luke."

"Wait, Syncere. Who is he?" she asked, smiling a little.

I gave a smile of my own. "He's a friend."

She looked at me skeptically. "That it?"

"Yes. Get your stuff," I said before leaving her room.

When I walked into the living room, Luke was walking back into the house. By himself.

"Where did he go?"

"I woke him up and kicked him in the ass. Told him if he ever bothered her again, I would shoot him."

"I told him the same thing the last time I saw him."

"He did this before?"

"Yeah. And I tuned his ass up."

"Well, maybe the second time is the charm."

"I'm ready," Trinity said, popping up behind us. Luke looked from her to me.

"She's staying with me for a couple of days. Luke, this is my cousin Trinity. Trinity, this is Luke," I introduced them.

"Hey, Trinity. Nice to meet you. So, y'all are cousins, huh? I swear y'all could pass for mother and daughter."

Shit!

J-Blunt

Chapter 23

I hated looking at Pistol's suburban. As time went by, dealing with Pistol's death got easier, but I still didn't like being reminded of his existence. Like I was being now.

After parking, I climbed the steps to Shay's house and rang the doorbell. I was picking up Latia. I planned on spending a few hours with her. I also wanted to introduce her to a special someone. I waited a few seconds, and when the door opened, I stared into the eyes of Shay.

"Hey, Luke," Shay said, looking genuinely happy to see me.

She had been like this the last few times I had come over. My choking her and threatening her had done something. In all the years I had known her, she had never been as respectful as she had been since our encounter. I figured she actually thought I killed Pistol, and the thought of me committing a murder had scared her straight.

"Hey, Shay. Is Latia ready?"

"Yeah. You want to come in?"

"Nah. Just tell her I'm out here," I said, staying on the porch. The last time I stepped foot in her house, things got out of hand. We didn't need a repeat.

"Latia! Your father is here!" Shay called as she went into the house.

Latia came bouncing out a few moments later. "Hi, Daddy."

"Hey, baby girl," I said as I bent down to kiss her. "Ready to go?"

"Yep. Where are we going?" she asked, grabbing my hand as I led her to my truck.

"I want you to meet somebody."

"Who? Where is she at?" she asked as I opened the door

and helped her climb in.

"How do you know it's a her?"

"It better be. Plus, you never asked me to meet none of your man friends."

"You way too smart for seven. I don't know what I'ma do with you."

"You'll continue to love me. So, who is she?"

"You'll see, Miss Know-It-All."

During the drive, me and Latia made small talk and sang along with Beyoncé. When I pulled into the parking lot of our destination, I went over to help her out of the truck. We held hands as we walked across the lot.

"What is this going to be?" Latia asked, looking at the workers who were renovating the building. The building she was talking about was an old store that was being changed into an office/studio.

"Read the sign," I said, pointing to a small, block-lettered sign hanging in front of a tarp-covered storefront window.

"Synful Desires? What does that mean?"

I thought for a second, searching for an explanation. I could not think of one appropriate enough for her seven-year-old ears. "Ask me that again in about ten years. For now, let's focus on who is inside the building."

When we walked into the building, men were at work in every inch of space. Some on ladders, some painting, and some on their knees messing with electrical outlets. I led Latia through the construction and toward the back of the building. There were five offices in the back. When I found the office I was looking for, I gave a couple of knocks on the door.

"Come in."

I walked in and seen Syncere sitting behind her desk. Trinity and a man I had never seen before were sitting in chairs across from her. It looked like they were looking over pictures spread across her desk.

"Hey, Syn. I didn't know you were busy. We were in the area, so I thought I'd stop by to say hi."

"Is that who I think it is?" Syncere asked, ignoring my explanation and eyeing Latia as she walked over to us.

"Yeah. Everybody, this is my daughter, Latia. Latia, this is Syncere, Trinity, and I'm sorry, man, but I don't know who you are," I told the stranger.

"I'm Shock. I'm a photographer," he introduced himself.

"'Sup, Shock. Nice to meet you."

"Aw, you are so cute!" Syn beamed, cutting off me and Shock's introduction.

"Thank you," Latia said, acting a little shy.

"I've been waiting to meet you. Your father has told me so much about you. How are you doing?"

"Fine."

"You sure are. Hey, did your father tell you I was starting a modeling company?"

"No."

"Well, I am. Ever thought about being a model?"

"No. I wanna be a veterinarian."

"Well, how about being a model and a vet? That would be fun, huh?"

"Yeah! Ooh, Daddy, can I be a model?" Latia asked, looking up at me like I had the keys to all her dreams.

"Sure, baby. You can be whatever you want to be. You know you creating a monster, right?" I asked, giving Syn the eye.

"No, I'm not. She is an angel. And I'm serious, Luke. I want to get her under contract. She is pretty."

"No problem. We'll talk about it later. I'ma let y'all get back to work and spend some time with my baby girl. What time you leaving here?"

"Couple hours. I have to make some more calls and go through a few stacks of paperwork. Trinity is still new to this, so I gotta be hands-on."

"A'ight. Call me when you wrap things up," I said, turning
to leave.

"Hey, hey, hey. Wait," Syn stopped me.

"Yeah."

"Aren't you forgetting something?" she asked, placing a hand on her hip and raising an eyebrow.

I knew what she wanted. "My bad." I could feel all the eyes in the room on us as our lips met.

"I'll call you as soon as I'm done. How about we stay in tonight. A Netflix night. My place," she said after we came up for air.

"Sounds good. Hit me up."

"Bye, Luke. Bye, Latia," Syncere called behind us.

"Is she your girlfriend?" Latia asked as we walked through the studio.

"Something like that."

And that was the truth. Although me and Syn hung out like we were in a relationship, we never spoke about making it official. I knew our feelings for each other were strong, but why we never talked about being together was beyond me. I figured she was probably waiting on me to bring it up.

"What do you mean, 'something like that'? Either she is or she isn't."

"We're headed in that direction. Is that good enough for you?"

"No. I think she should be your girlfriend. I like her. And she's pretty.

Even though my daughter was a kid, her opinion meant a

lot to me. Having her approval of Syn brought me one step closer to making us official.

"I like her, too."

***

After taking Latia to the movies and shopping, I dropped her off at home and went to find Trigga. It had been a couple of days since the last time I'd seen him, and I wanted to grill him on a couple of things. Namely, how did he kill so easily? Almost a month had gone by since I had listened to him shoot Pistol and I shot the man in Syn's club. I thought the passage of time would stop my nightmares, but it hadn't. They stopped being as frequent, but I still had them.

"Cool-Hand Luke! 'Sup, nigga?" Trigga greeted me, giving me a half-hug as we shook hands. I had found him in his hood on 37th and Center. We were standing next to his candy-red 2012 Audi A8 that sat on 22" chrome wheels.

"What up, Trigga?"

"Shit. Just out here posted on the block. You know I gotta come through here every now and then so muthafuckas know I ain't dead or in jail. You know the streets love to talk about a nigga's downfalls. One of these niggas'd love to take my spot," he said as he pulled a blunt from the pocket of his dark designer jeans.

"I hear you, man. Hey, I wanted to run something by you," I said, looking around to make sure no one was in earshot.

"Go 'head, nigga," he said, pulling out a lighter. Clouds of weed smoke billowed in the air as he puffed hard at the flame until the blunt was lit.

"The first time you ever killed somebody, did you have nightmares?"

Trigga looked at me suspiciously. I had never asked him about murder before, and I could see the millions of questions floating around in his mind. "Why you askin' me that?"

"Because, man. I been havin' nightmares."

"About Pistol?"

"Yeah."

Trigga was silent for a few moments. I could tell he was thinking. Remembering.

"Luke, that shit fucked me up for years, my nigga," he mumbled before taking a long drag on his blunt.

His answer surprised me. I thought he killed without a conscience. "For real?"

"Hell yeah. My first time, I fucked around and had to kill a nigga we grew up wit'. Remember Champion?"

I thought for a few moments. We went to middle school with a dude named Champion. I heard he got killed while I was away in college. "Dawg, you killed Champion?" I asked, unable to contain my surprise.

"I had to. He robbed one of Big Chief spots. I had just joined Chief team, and he chose me to lay down the law. I can still hear that nigga's pleas. Shit was fucked up. But I was a young nigga lookin' for a meal. And Chief made sure I never went hungry.

"Damn." That was all I could say. I couldn't imagine killing somebody I grew up with.

"So, Pistol won't go away, huh?"

"Not just him."

"Who else?" Trigga asked, staring me down. I hadn't told him about the shooting in Syn's club.

"I killed somebody about a month ago. Shot him, like, nine or ten times."

"What? You bullshittin'! You offed a nigga, and you just

now tellin' me?" Trigga asked, looking at me like I had just told him I knew where Jimmy Hoffa was buried.

"Man, I wasn't trying to tell nobody. Shit scared the hell out of me. But I had to do it. He was choking Syn and going for his gun. I just started squeezing the trigger."

A look of alarm spread across Trigga's face. "Wait. Who the fuck is Syn? You left a witness, nigga?"

"Syncere is this chick I'm seeing. She owns that strip club you got the girls for yo' party from. The Den of Syn."

"Wait, wait, wait. You fuckin' that badass bitch and you didn't tell me? And now you goin' to war over this ho? Too many secrets, my nigga."

"C'mon, Trigga. Chill with the name callin'," I defended Syncere. To Trigga, every woman except his mother was a bitch or a ho. I didn't want him to think of Syn like that.

"And you in love wit' this bitch? I mean, her?"

"It ain't like that, Trigga. We just cool. I just happened to show up when they was robbing her. I whooped one of them and took his pistol. Then, when I ran in the office. You know."

Trigga busted out laughing. "My nigga on some Tom Cruise shit!" he yelled. "So, who was the niggas? What happened with the nigga you whooped? You off him, too?"

"Nah. He got away. Don't know who they were, either. The one I killed, we fed to some pigs. Syn thought of that. I wanted to call the police and scream self-defense."

"Damn, Luke. She sound gangsta. That's my kinda bitch. I mean, broad."

"Yeah. She cool."

"So, you seein' the nigga you offed in yo' dreams, huh?

"Yeah. Him and Pistol. I don't have the dreams as much as I used to, but they still come every now and then."

"On the real, Luke, I don't know no remedy for that shit.

Just gotta let time do its thang. You know what's crazy? I done murked a lot of muthafuckas, but the only one I ever see in my sleep in Champ. Crazy, huh?"

"Man, this whole conversation sounds crazy," I laughed.

"Yeah. I guess you right. But this killin' shit is all I know. Don't get too deep in this street shit, Luke. You got a choice, my nigga. Sounds like you had to kill the nigga you whacked, but don't get too deep in this shit. You spent yo' whole life dodgin' the streets. Don't get in them now. And watch yo' back. Y'all let that nigga get away, and he probably gon' come back. You got a strap?"

"Yeah. Went and copped one right after that shit with Pistol."

"Good. Stay strapped. Muthafuckas out here playin' for keeps. What the nigga that got away look like? I can put my feelers out to see who he is."

"A built, Samoan, karate-knowing dude. Like, size three or size four. Looked like he just got out the joint. Long hair. And like I said, he know karate. Probably got a few cuts on his face. I fucked him up pretty bad."

"A long-haired, karate-knowin' Samoan. Damn, Luke. That sound like some professional shit. Niggas in the hood don't know karate. You sure he was trynna rob her?" he asked, sounding just as skeptical as I had when Syn told me they were robbers.

"Yeah. That's what she told me."

"A'ight. I'ma put my ear to the street and see what I can dig up. Make sure you keep that burner on you, nigga."

"Yeah. I will. This my new American Express Card."

Chapter 24

I stared at the headstone, wishing like I did every single day that they would come back to me. And by 'they' I was talking about my parents, Fred and Sandra Staples. They had been gone for almost twenty years. A few months after I got locked up for killing Rasheed, they were killed in a car accident. I still wonder if it was some kind of karma that took them. A kind of atoning for Rasheed's death. Whatever the reason they were gone, I still had the empty spot in my soul that missed them. Had they been around, not only would my prison experience been different, but my daughter wouldn't have grown up in the system.

I had lost so much, and just when it looked like things were getting better for me, it had all changed. I had developed a relationship with my daughter, found a man who would literally kill to protect me, and my business and investments were turning profits. Then Calico showed up.

I stared down at the patch of dirt that held my parents, trying to figure out my next move with Luke, Trinity, and Calico. I wanted to tell Luke how I felt about him and take things to the next level, but that meant I would have to tell him about going to prison, killing Rasheed, Trinity being my daughter, and Calico coming after me for the money. Those were a lot of secrets to expose in one conversation. And I still wasn't sure how to bring it all up. Nor was I sure how he would react. But one thing was for sure: if I wanted him to be my man, I would have to tell him everything.

Then there was Trinity. I felt bad for lying to her, and I knew whenever the truth came out, it would probably do more harm than good. I knew I needed to tell her the truth, but I didn't know how. I had gotten so used to lying and manipulating that it seemed second nature. Now my secretive nature threatened to hurt the two most important people in my life.

And then there was Calico. I knew I hadn't seen the last of him. He was serious about his money. There was no doubt in my mind he would be reaching out to me. And since Luke had killed one of his goons, I knew he wouldn't be coming to talk.

And this brought me back to square one. Luke. To ensure my safety and his, I would have to tell him everything. And we would have to put our heads together and try to find a solution. I hoped.

My phone's vibration pulled me from my thoughts. I pulled it from my purse and looked at the screen. It was Luke.

"Hey, baby. I was just thinking about you."

"Funny, because I was just thinking about you, too. You wanna revisit that conversation about destiny? Tell Jayda it's real?"

"Forget Jayda. I want to see you."

"That's why I'm calling. I'm leaving work now. Where are you?"

"I'm visiting my parents' grave. I've been doing some soul-searching. I want to talk to you. I have some things I need to tell you."

"Sounds important. How about we meet at your place?"

"Okay. See you then."

During the drive home, I stewed over how Luke might react to everything I was about to tell him. No matter how many ways I tried to tell him, in my visions he always got mad and left me. I didn't want that to happen. I didn't know what I would do if he actually left.

When I turned onto my block, I seen Luke's truck at the stop sign to my right, about to turn behind me. We had arrived at my house at almost the same time. I thought back to what he had just said about destiny. It made me wonder if everything that was happening to us was destined. And if so, did that mean he would accept my baggage?

After I pulled into my driveway, Luke pulled in behind me. We got out of our vehicles at the same time. I was walking toward him to get a kiss when I noticed the black minivan. It was parked across the street from my house. I don't know why I noticed it, but I did. And I got a funny feeling.

"That was crazy how we got here at the same time, huh?" Luke was saying as we closed the distance.

I didn't answer him. I was giving all of my attention to the minivan. The sliding door was opening, and I was looking to see who would get out.

When Luke noticed me watching something behind him, he turned to look.

When the van's door fully opened, the tall Hawaiian from my club got out carrying one of the biggest guns I had ever seen. Another man with a gun just as big came from the other side.

"Shit!" I screamed, going for my purse.

"Move!" Luke screamed, pushing me to the ground just as the Hawaiian started shooting.

I could hear the bullets tearing into Luke's truck as I crawled around the front. When the other man began shooting, it sounded like we were being attacked by an entire army. Both of them had fully automatic machine guns, and the bullets sounded like they were tearing Luke's truck apart. I pulled my .380 from my purse and stayed low. I was terrified. They had two big guns with a lot of bullets, and all I had was a handgun with ten bullets. I didn't see a way out of this, but I didn't plan on going out without a fight.

I stayed low, almost underneath the truck, and watched the men's feet. The shooting had stopped, but they were walking toward the truck, one walking toward the back, the other coming around my side. And I didn't see Luke. I knew they had shot him. Problem was, I didn't see his body.

Then the thought of Luke running off and leaving me jumped into my mind. If he ran and left me, I wouldn't have to worry about confessing anything to him. If I survived, I was going to hunt him down and cut off his balls.

The sound of rocks crunching under someone's foot forced me to abandon my thoughts of castrating Luke. The guy moving toward my side of the truck was getting closer. I knew if I let them corner me, I was dead. I crawled further under the truck and pointed my gun at the set of legs closest to me. I didn't know who I was about to shoot, but it didn't matter. They were both trying to kill me.

Pop-pop-pop-pop-pop! I fired.

"Aw, shit!" he screamed and began jumping in the air.

I heard something inside the truck move, then more shooting.

Boom-boom-boom-boom!

I crawled from under the truck and seen Luke kneeling in the front seat, shooting out his back window. I looked to where the man who was walking behind the truck had been. He was gone. His gun was on the ground. I looked around and seen the Hawaiian man in a limp-run toward the minivan. The other man was running in the same direction, holding what looked like a dead arm.

Luke got out of the truck and continued shooting at the van as it sped away. He didn't stop until his gun was empty.

"C'mon, Luke! We have to go!" I screamed, running around to get into the passenger seat of his truck. I wanted to take my car, but Luke's truck had me boxed in.

"They had on bulletproof vests, Syn. I shot that muthafucka in his chest, and he didn't fall," Luke said as he sped away.

I didn't speak. I was too busy looking around, watching our front and back.

"Who the fuck was that, Syn?"

"I don't know who they are, Luke. I–"

"Don't give me that bullshit. That was that Hawaiian nigga. What the fuck you got me into?" he yelled, looking at me angrily. His eyes were red and bulging. Thick veins popped out of his neck and around his temples. I hadn't seen this side of him before. When he shot the man in my office, he was scared. Panicked. Now it looked like he had outgrown that incident. It looked like the accountant had died and a real gangsta was born.

"The reason I told you to come over was because I wanted to tell you everything. I don't know who they are, but–"

"You wanna fuck wit' me, Syn? Well, cool. Fuck wit' me!" Luke yelled, smashing the brakes and bringing the truck to a screeching stop on the side of the road.

"What the fuck are you doing?" I panicked.

"You wanna fuck wit' me now, I'ma fuck wit' chu. Start talkin'!"

"Baby, chill. I'm about to tell you everything. That's why I told you to come over. Drive, Luke. Drive."

He gave me a long stare before pulling away.

"A couple of weeks ago, a man named Calico came to my club talking about I owe him some money."

"How much?"

"$100,000. Plus interest."

He looked at me like I had just told him I was pregnant with Jesus. "A hundred G's?"

"One hundred and sixty thousand. He wants interest."

He shook his head. "What the fuck you got me in, Syn?"

"I didn't know he would send guys to try to kill me, or that people would die. I thought he was trying to scare me."

"Why does he want this money? For what?"

"Just listen. Don't say anything."

When he didn't speak, I began.

"I just got out of prison about a year and a half ago."

"What? For what?" he screamed.

"Just listen, Luke. Please. You're the first person I'm telling this. I just need you to hear me out."

He gave me a long stare before turning back to watch the road.

"I went to prison for murder."

"You gotta be fucking kidding me," Luke mumbled, shaking his head. I could tell he was holding back. I knew he wanted to scream and shout, but he was letting me have the floor.

"In 1995, I killed my friend's boyfriend. He was trying to rape me. It all started after my boyfriend, C-Money, got locked up. The Feds came and took everything we owned. I didn't want to go home to my parents and listen to their 'I-told-you-so's and 'that's-what-you-get-for-messing-with-a-drug-dealer', so I moved in with my friend and her man. One day I let her talk me into having a threesome. I didn't want to do it, but her and her man were taking care of me, so I kind of felt like I owed them. So I did it. Then Rasheed started wanting me by myself. He threatened to put me out if I didn't have sex with him. I was young and poor, so I felt like I didn't have a choice. Pretty soon we started having sex on a regular, and he started calling me his bitch.

"C-Money was eventually found guilty for ordering the murder of a police officer, and he snapped out in court. He shot a bailiff before they killed him. Watching him die put me in a serious battle with depression, but Rasheed didn't care. He wanted sex. I denied him, and he tried to rape me. We fought, and I ended up stabbing him. When I realized what I had done, I panicked. I didn't think to call the police. I just grabbed his money and ran.

"I was on the run for three months. I got caught because I missed my mom. When I went to see her, the police were waiting. They had been watching the house. Charged me with First Degree Murder. I told them he tried to rape me, but they weren't hearing me. Because I ran. I went to trial and was found guilty of Second Degree Murder. Got 25 years. Did 17. I had locked the money in a safety deposit box and buried the key. When I got out, it was still there.

"Now Calico shows up and starts saying the money I took from Rasheed was his. And he wants it back."

"Why didn't you tell me all of this before? You got me killing and having shootouts in the middle of the day. I didn't want this shit in my life."

"It was in my past, Luke. I didn't know all of this would happen."

"Why didn't you just pay Calico, or whatever his name is? I could've traded in some stock and sold some bonds. You have almost $250,000 in your portfolio."

"I don't know. I thought he was bluffing and trying to extort me. I didn't know all this would happen, that we would have to feed people to pigs and have shootouts."

"Dammit, Syn! You should've told me all of this shit. About your past and the money. We probably could've avoided all this."

"I know. You're right. And I'm sorry I didn't tell you. But I didn't trust you then. I wasn't sure you would be able to handle all of my baggage. Wasn't sure you would understand. You're a college grad. A working guy. Never been in trouble. I didn't want to taint you and bring you into my world."

"Well, I'm in it now. And I don't feel as square as I used to."

Silence filled the cab of the truck. I knew he was thinking about everything I had just said, and I didn't want to disturb the process. I had to let him process everything.

"I'ma be honest, Syn," Luke spoke up a few moments later. "I don't want to be in this shit. I really don't. But I gave you my word, and I'ma keep it. But, before we go any further, is there anything else I need to know? Anything at all?"

I knew now was my time to get it all out. "Yes. My real name is Loretta Staples. And Trinity is not really my cousin. She is my daughter. C-Money is her father. She was a few months old when I went to jail, so my parents took custody of her. She was in the car with my parents when they died, but she survived. Since we had no next of kin, they put her in the system. When I got out, I found her. I was too scared to tell her I was her mother, so I told her I was C-Money's cousin."

"And that's all?" he asked, looking at me suspiciously.

"Yes. That's everything."

"Okay. We will deal with Trinity later. For now, let's worry about Calico and getting out of this truck. I need to make a call. I have a friend who could probably help us."

Chapter 25

"Luke! What the fuck happened, nigga?" Trigga asked after I pulled my truck into the garage. We were on 38th and Chambers, at one of his hiding spots.

"I know who they is," I said as I climbed from the truck.

"Who the fuck is they, and what the fuck they have?" he asked, eyeing the damage.

I turned to see what he was looking at. There were about 20 or 30 holes the size of 50-cent pieces spread throughout the driver's side of my truck. It looked like I had driven through a war zone.

"Calico."

The look on Trigga's face let me know just how deep the shit was that we were in. His eyes bulged, and I thought I seen a hint of worry flash in his eyes.

"You mean Calico? Big money Calico?"

"Yeah. Him," Syn answered as she climbed from the truck.

Trigga eyed her, noticing her for the first time. "Well, if it ain't the devil herself."

"Syn, Trigga. Trigga, Syn," I introduced them.

"So, you the one that got my nigga from behind the desk to pullin' triggas."

"He's more than capable," Syn sassed.

Trigga laughed. "Yeah, Luke. You gon' have yo' hands full wit' dis one."

"Trigga, I need a car. And who the fuck is Calico?" I asked.

"Shit, Calico practically run the streets, my nigga. When Big Chief left, Calico took over all the blocks, spots, and operations he left. Calico's money is long. Shit, he hired me to do a couple of moves for him. Havin' a beef wit' Calico ain't good, fam. He connected. To everybody. Police, politicians, businesses, the streets."

"I gotta get him off our asses, Trigga."

"This shit don't make no sense, Luke. You sayin' Calico tried to rob her? Why? His money too long. What, she got a couple mil or somethin'?" Trigga asked, eyeing Syn.

I looked over at Syn to see if she had anything to say. She looked unsure, so I spoke up for her.

"Calico didn't send his people to rob her. It was a collection call. He sent them to have her sign a contract to give him more than half of the equity in her club."

"Damn, Syn. What the fuck you got my nigga in?" Trigga asked, looking her up and down like she stank.

"It ain't like that, Trigga. Some shit happened back in the day, and Calico sayin' she owe him a hundred and sixty thousand dollars."

A look of astonishment flashed in Trigga's eyes. "A hundred sixty G's. For real?"

"Yeah," Syn affirmed.

"Shit, for a hundred G's, I'll kill the nigga whole family."

The look in Trigga's eyes told me how serious he was. I was tempted to tell Syn to pay him and unleash Trigga and his Trigga Klan upon Calico, but I didn't want any more bloodshed. "I want to find a way to end this without nobody else dying. We already know Calico has connections since he found out where Syn lives. He probably gon' find out where I live soon, if he hasn't already. We gotta figure out a way to bring this to an end. Soon. And with as little deaths as possible."

We all went into deep thought for a few moments.

"Did you holla at Chief? He still got pull out here," Trigga offered.

I seen a light flash behind Syn's eyes. She liked Trigga's idea. I didn't. The last thing I wanted to do was tell my brother I had killed and one of the biggest players in the city was after me. Chief did his best to keep me from the mean streets. I didn't want to tell him I was damn near knee-deep in them.

But as I stared into Syn and Trigga's faces and weighed my options, it seemed as if I didn't have a choice.

***

I stared at the clock on the wall as I sat at the conference table. I didn't really care about the clock or the time. I was staring at it because I needed something to focus on. I didn't want to look at the other two faces in the room, and the clock's second hand gave me something to focus on to keep my mind off what I knew was impending doom.

I was beyond nervous for a lot of reasons. My life had changed drastically in the last few weeks. I had gone from counting money to counting how many bullets I could fit in the clip of my gun. My life had become a roller coaster ride. There was no telling what would happen next. I didn't like that kind of uncertainty.

But what I didn't like more than the uncertainty of my new life was having to explain it all to Barron. The reason for my bad nerves.

"You okay?" Syn asked, pulling me from my thoughts. She was seated next to me.

"Yeah. I'm good," I lied.

"He should be out in a few minutes," April spoke up. April Bently was one of my brother's attorneys. She had pulled some strings to get me and Syn in to see Barron. Syn wasn't on Barron's visiting list, so I had to go through his lawyer to get us in to see him. I didn't know the details behind the strings she pulled, nor did I care. The important thing was we were there.

When I heard the doorknob on the other side of the door turn, I looked up. The door swung open, and in walked Barron. All six feet, 235 pounds of him. He wore a tan-khaki suit and white Nikes. Even though I was nervous about seeing him, I couldn't wipe the smile from my face.

"Barron! What up, big bro?" I smiled as I stood to greet him.

"Luke? 'Sup, boy? What is goin' on?" he asked as we hugged.

"I'ma fill you in in a second. This is Syncere. Syncere, this is my brother, Big Chief."

Syn stood to shake his hand. "Nice to meet you. I've heard a lot about you."

"Oh, yeah? Well, I can't say the same," Barron replied, cutting his eyes at me.

I hadn't been able to tell him anything about Syn. I hadn't seen him in a few months, and when we talked on the phone, she never came up.

"She's a good friend, Barron. She's good."

"Okay. You look familiar. Where do I know you from?" Barron asked, eyeing Syn.

"I don't know. It might be my face. I was out of commission for awhile."

"Nah, I've seen you somewhere before, I'm sure. I never forget a face. It will come to me," he told Syn before turning to his lawyer. "Hey, April. Nice to see you again. Now, tell me why y'all are here. What is this emergency?"

"Hi, Barron. I don't know the emergency. That is their problem. I am just the third party. But I do want to let you all know everything that is said here is protected under attorney-client privilege. Nothing said here can be used in court. Shall we all have seats and discuss why we are here?" April asked, looking around the room.

We all took her cue and had seats. Barron sat directly across from me.

"So, what's goin' on, Luke?" Barron asked, giving me one of my father's intense stares.

"I'm in some shit, Barron. I need you to talk to Calico for me."

He blinked a couple of times like he couldn't understand what I had just said.

"You mean light-skinned Calico? My nigga from back in the day?"

"Yeah. Him," I nodded.

"How do you know Calico? Why do you need me to talk to him? What you done got yo'self into?" he asked, looking back and forth from me to Syn.

I took a deep breath before spilling the beans. "I killed one of his guys and shot another one. Syn shot one, too."

The look on Barron's face spoke louder than his words. He looked like he was living out his worst nightmare. The look in his eyes showed utter disbelief. Then it changed to anger. For a moment I thought he was about to get out of his chair and try to fight me.

"Wait. Hold on. You shot somebody? When the fuck did you even get a gun? You mean you killed somebody? For real?"

"I took it from some Hawaiian dude I knocked out. They were trying to extort Syn. It all happened quick. I didn't have time to think. It was either me or him."

Barron just stared at me. Didn't say a word, just stared. I could see the disappointment in his eyes. And hurt. And even a little bit of fear for my safety.

"Shit, Luke. I can't believe you tellin' me this shit. I tried to keep you away from the streets, and you fucked around and got in them anyway."

The room became silent again. No one spoke or moved. I knew it was hard for him to digest what I just told him. All of my life I had been a playboy and sports jock. Now I was telling him of shootings and murder.

"So, why is Calico trying to extort you?" Barron asked, glaring at Syn angrily. I could see the dislike for her in his eyes.

"He thinks I owe him some money."

"Do you?"

"He thinks I do."

"Listen, Syncere. Quit bullshittin' me. You got my li'l brother in some shit, and I'm trynna help," Barron snapped.

Syn looked over at me. I nodded.

"About eighteen years ago I killed this guy named Rasheed and took some money. $100,000. Ca–"

"Oh, shit! You killed Sheed? That's you?" Barron cut her off. Syn nodded. "That's where I know you from. You used to fuck wit' my nigga C-Money. Yeah, I remember you now. Shit. Small world. But go ahead. I didn't mean to cut you off."

"Yeah, well, Calico is saying the money I took from Rasheed was his."

"Sheed used to work for Calico. That was his money you took."

"So, what are our options, Barron. Can you help us?" I cut in.

"I don't know, Luke. She gotta give that money back. And now that y'all spilled some of his niggas' blood, it might be worse. When I go back to the block, I'ma make some calls. See if I can get a favor. But don't leave town until I call you. Stay in that hotel until you hear from me," Barron warned, standing to his feet. The visit was over.

"Okay," I agreed.

"Thanks for getting them in, April." He hugged his attorney.

"No problem. Call me if you need anything."

"Thanks for helping us out, bro," I said, walking over to hug Barron.

He whispered in my ear as we embraced, "Listen, Luke. Get the fuck away from that bitch. She is bad news. She tainted."

Our eyes locked as we broke the embrace. His stare was hard. Serious.

"Sorry we had to meet under these circumstances, Big Chief. But thanks for everything," Syn said as she walked over to me and Barron.

"It's nothing, Syncere. I will do anything for family."

***

"You've been quiet all night. What's on your mind?" Syn asked. We were back at the hotel, lying in bed and watching BET. Reruns of *Martin* were on.

"I been thinking about my brother. It's been a few months since I seen him. I hate that I can walk in and out of that prison, but he can't," I said, giving her half of the truth. Truth was, I was thinking about my brother, but not about him leaving prison. I was thinking about what he had said about Syn. That she was bad news. That she was tainted. I wanted to defend her, wanted to make some excuses, but I couldn't. The last few weeks of my life had given proof to my brother's claims. In a matter of days I had gone from a nine-to-five guy to carrying guns and murder. I never thought I would end up in the position I was in. And I was in so deep it was hard to see a way out.

"He's probably thinking the same thing right now. I hated being in prison. I hated the monotony. I hated that I couldn't do what I wanted when I wanted."

"Yeah. I don't know what that's like, and hopefully we can avoid me finding out."

"I think your brother can help us. It still seems like he has juice out here. I can tell he used to be somebody big."

"Yeah. Hopefully. I really want my life back."

"I'm sorry I got you into this, Luke. I didn't mean for this to get out of hand like this," Syn said, looking up at me with tears in her eyes.

Seeing her get this emotional surprised me. This was a first. All of her Superwoman powers were gone. She was vulnerable. And maybe even a little scared. Seeing her like this made me want to hold her. Console her. She had grown on me. I couldn't leave her if I wanted to. I had it bad.

"It's okay, Syn. We're here now. Together. And that's all that matters. Whatever happens, we'll face it. Together."

"You really mean that? Because if you want to get away from me, I would understand."

Her words had no conviction. I knew she didn't mean what she had said. She said those words because they sounded like the right things to say.

"I tried, Syn. And I can't. You have a hold on me. You remember when I was singing *You Got it Bad* in my truck that day?"

She nodded.

"I wasn't just singing that song, Syn. That's how I felt. That's why I'm still here. That's why I'm risking my life. I don't know how all this will end, but I know I wouldn't want to be anywhere else, nor would I want to be with anyone else. I'm falling in love with you, Syn."

I said it. I laid it all on the line.

Syn rolled on top of me and began staring into my eyes. It was like she was searching my soul. It felt weird, like we were connecting on a deeper level. Something spiritual. The tears that began flowing from her eyes dripped onto my face. I could taste the saltiness of them when she bent down to kiss me. The kiss was hard and passionate, like she was trying to say with her lips what she hadn't spoken verbally.

It wasn't long before we were naked. She stayed on top of me and we continued kissing as I entered her. We moaned as our bodies moved in a slow, perfect rhythm. It was sensual. Intimate. Like we were exchanging pieces of ourselves. For the first time in my life, I was making love. And it felt good. And we didn't rush. We cruised. Took our time. There were no plays for power. No games. Both of us were our true selves. We gave everything we had from the depths of our souls.

When her orgasm began building, she rode me faster, sucked my lips harder, and dug her nails into my shoulders. Everything felt perfect. Just right. And when she came, so did I. It was glorious.

Our lovemaking session was so explosive, there was no need for another round. She fell on top of me and lay there. I felt the sleep creeping up on me, but before my eyes closed for good, I memorized everything I could about the moment. Where we were, what I seen, how I felt, what I smelled. I wanted to remember this moment forever. I knew at that exact moment that I had found my destiny.

***

I was awakened the next morning by the sound of my

phone vibrating on the bedside table. "Hello?"

"Luke, it's me."

I recognized the voice instantly. It was Barron. I perked up and my eyes shot open.

"I talked to Calico."

Chapter 26

"Wow! These are some really good shots," I told Shock as I looked over the photographs he was showing me. We were in my office at my modeling agency, and Shock was showing me some of the work he had on his laptop. They were pictures of sexy women in multiple poses, all of them tastefully seductive. Just how I liked them.

"Glad you like. I was hoping the studio would be done soon. I can't wait to start working with the girls," he said eagerly, showing off his dentist-whitened smile.

Shock was alright in the looks department. Dark-skinned, short, and a little chubby with a short, neatly-cut afro. What he lacked physically, he made up with his wardrobe. He was always well-dressed. Today he wore a nicely-tailored, money-green suit.

"You'll be able to start work soon. They say another week or so and all the construction will be done. I can't wait 'til we are fully functional, too. I already got us some print deals."

"Damn. You work fast, boss lady."

"Time is money," I smiled.

"Fo' sho. I just wanted to show these to you. I'ma get back to my office and finish setting some things in order."

"Okay. I'll be here for a few more hours. Holler if you need anything."

When Shock left my office, I got back to my contracts and looking over some potential models' portfolios. I had been immersing myself in getting the modeling agency up and running since we had returned from seeing Luke's brother. For the past three days all I did was work, work, work. And for the last three nights, I made love to Luke, made love to Luke, and made love to Luke. The last time I felt this happy and complete was when I was pregnant with Trinity and living the lavish life with C-Money. But this time I didn't have to worry about a sad ending to my story.

According to Luke, Calico agreed to squash everything. Said something about Calico owing Big Chief some favors.

I felt good. At peace. And in love.

What I didn't like, however, was Luke's overprotectiveness. He had me holed-up in this modeling agency and forbade me to go to my club. He said he wanted me to wait a little while before going back to The Den of Syn to make sure Calico stayed true to his word. It annoyed me that Luke was being so overprotective, but I understood. We had spent the last month feeding people to pigs and dodging bullets. So, I put Jayda in charge of the club until Luke felt things were safe.

Another thing I wasn't too fond of was Luke making me move in with him. I hadn't been home since the shoot-out in my driveway. As far as Luke was concerned, my house didn't exist, and it was too dangerous to go back to. Again, I didn't like his decision, but I understood his concerns. He was my man now, and I knew he had my best interests at heart. I just had to trust him. Which was hard, since I wasn't used to other people making my decisions for me.

My thoughts of me, Luke, and my lifestyle changes were interrupted when another one of my lifestyle changes walked into my office. "When will you learn to knock?" I asked Trigga as I cut my eyes at him.

"I don't get paid to knock. Here. Luke on the phone," he said, holding out his phone for me.

At the mention of Luke, a smile spread across my face. "Hey, baby!"

"What up, girl? How is everything going?"

"Fine. Trying to get Trigga to act like he has home

training. For some reason he won't knock on the door before he enters a room."

"I don't even think he knows how to knock. He don't need to in his line of work," Luke joked.

"Yeah, I hear you. But if he gon' be my bodyguard, then I'ma have to send him to obedience school."

"See, you got jokes, Syn. I ain't no fuckin' dog," Trigga said, staring down at me.

"You betta stop before you piss him off!" Luke laughed.

"Well, the next time he better knock," I told Luke, ignoring Trigga's stare.

"Hey, I'm about to wrap up in a few minutes. You staying late tonight?"

"No. I'll be heading out in an hour or two. Got a few more portfolios to look at."

"A'ight. I'ma see you at home, then. I love you."

Hearing Luke say those words made something melt on the inside of me. We had been confessing our love for only three days, but I swear it sounded better every time we said it. It sounded like destiny.

"I love you, too, baby," I sang.

"A'ight. Let me holla back at Trigga."

"Okay. Here. He wants you."

After handing the phone back to Trigga, I watched and listened to Trigga's side of the conversation.

"Yeah. A'ight. Whatever, nigga! You trippin'. A'ight. Love."

"What did he say?" I asked after Trigga hung up the phone. I wanted to know the rest of their conversation.

"For you to hook me up wit' Trinity fine ass. Cuzzo is feelin' me. Let me in that family tree."

"Boy, please! Get out of my office before I hurt you!" I yelled, throwing my pen at him.

He laughed as he left.

I stayed at the modeling agency for another hour before I decided to leave. When I walked into the waiting room, Trigga and his friend Stan had their faces buried in their phones. Luke had insisted I have around-the-clock protection. So, if I wasn't with him, Trigga and one of his Trigga Klan members watched over me.

"I'm ready, y'all," I told them.

"'Bout time. Damn. I know I'm due for some overtime after sittin' here for six hours," Trigga complained as he got up and stretched.

"On the real. Got my hos puttin' APBs out on me an' shit," Stan added.

"Technically y'all still owe me another hour of services. It's only four. I normally leave at five. So, if y'all wanna chill a li'l longer, we can," I teased them.

"Damn, Syn. You always gotta try to one-up a nigga. You bet not be bossin' my nigga Luke around. You one of them dominant females. I'ma have to teach Luke how to handle yo' types."

"Ain't no handlin' my type, Trigga. I'm rare, baby. You ain't neva met a woman like me. And don't worry about Luke. He's in good hands. Now, let's get up outta here. I wanna meet him at home."

"Yo, Syn. You should let me be a model scout," Trigga said as we left the building.

"What? You don't know the first thing about scouting. We need photogenic girls, not jump-offs."

"Shit, I don't discriminate. Plus, all them model hos be jump-offs. Put me in the room wit' a model chic and I'm smashin'. Guaranteed. And I got the footage to prove it. Wanna see?"

"No, Trigga. I'm good. You can keep your porn to

yourself," I told him as we neared the black Lincoln Town Car I had rented.

"Nah, Syn. It ain't like that. I'm–" he was saying, but stopped.

I looked up at him to see why he had stopped talking. He was staring across the parking lot. A black suburban was speeding toward us. I clutched my purse to my chest. My .380 was inside.

"Who is that?"

"I don't know. Here. Get in the car and start it up," Trigga said, handing me the keys as he shoved me into the car.

I reached into the front seat and started the car before lying across the back seat and pulling out my gun. Trigga and Stan also pulled out guns. Trigga had two big, black automatic handguns. Stan had a big, shiny revolver.

When I heard the tires on the suburban screech, I lifted my head high enough to see out the window. The SUV was about twenty feet from the sedan. Three men I had never seen before got out. They all had really big guns. And then Calico got out.

What the fuck?

"Trigga, this not yo' fight, killa. She owes me. I need to collect." Calico said.

I felt sick to my stomach. What the fuck was he talking about? Luke said everything was squashed.

"You gotta charge that shit to the game, Calico. She like my sister, fam. I can't turn my back on my family," Trigga responded.

"Don't bite the hand that fed you over pussy, nigga. This shit ain't worth yo' life," Calico warned.

"My life ain't on the line," Trigga retorted.

"Trigga, yo' people work for me. This whole fuckin' city

works for me. Do you know how I found you?" Calico asked.

I had been wondering that myself. Luke had me at the agency because it wasn't listed yet. There was no way Calico should have known where I was.

"I don't give a fuck how you knew. All I know is I can't let you touch her."

"So, you really wanna die over her, huh? A'ight. No problem. Stan, kill him," Calico ordered.

I looked up at Stan just in time to see him raise his gun to Trigga's face. He squeezed the trigger. The gun clicked, but there was no boom. When Stan realized what had happened, a look of terror spread across his face. Like he knew death was certain.

Without missing a beat, Trigga lifted one of his guns and shot Stan in the face. Before Stan's body could fall to the ground, Trigga turned his guns on Calico and company. I rolled onto the floor of the sedan as the gunfight ensued. It sounded like the Fourth of July.

A few moments later, the driver's side door opened. I pointed my gun toward the door, ready to shoot, and almost shot Trigga.

"Fuckin' bitch-ass niggas shot me!" he yelled as he slammed the car in drive and sped away.

"What? Where?" I asked, jumping into the front seat to have a look.

"It ain't shit, Syn. Move. I'm good," Trigga groaned, pushing me away. He had on a black t-shirt, so I couldn't tell if he was bleeding.

"Why is he still looking for me? I thought he was leaving us alone," I asked as I focused my attention on our surroundings. We were speeding out of the parking lot, and I was keeping my eyes out for the police or another ambush.

"He want you, Syn. We. Uh!" Trigga coughed, spitting blood all over the steering wheel and dashboard. It looked like he had coughed up one of his organs.

"Where are you shot at? Let me see," I yelled, reaching out to touch him. Trigga pushed me away again, but not before I was able to put a hand on his chest. It was sticky and wet. When I looked at my hand, it was covered in blood.

"I told you I was good. I gotta getchu outta here. I only hit two of 'em. Calico and one of dem niggas is still back there."

"But, Trigga, you're–" I was saying when the back window exploded. I screamed and ducked in the seat as bullets tore into the car.

"Get dem niggas off our ass!" Trigga yelled, ducking down in the seat as he smashed the gas.

I grabbed my .380 and spun toward the shattered back window. The suburban was gaining on us. Someone was hanging out the passenger window, shooting. I aimed at the truck's windshield and began squeezing the trigger. I didn't stop until all ten of my bullets were gone.

The SUV turned off onto a side street. "They're gone. We have to get you to a hospital."

"Nah, fuck that. If I let them keep me alive, they gon' send me to jail forever," Trigga grimaced.

"Trigga, you're hurt. You gotta get help. Pull over," I said, pulling out my cell phone.

"Syn, don't do that shit. Don't call for help. I'm not goin' to jail."

I stopped dialing and stared at him as he pulled the car over. It looked like the life was being drained out of him. I could see him getting weaker by the moment. "Trigga, you gon' die. You have to get help."

"Fuck that shit, Syn. We all gotta go one day. I'm goin'

out on my own. Let me die a gangsta," he whispered as he struggled to put the car in park.

"But they can save you. You don't have to die like this."

"I ain't finna let them crackers bury me. If they keep me alive. I'ma spend the rest of my life dyin' slow. I ain't dyin' in the joint."

I wanted to argue with him. I wanted to ignore what he said and call for help. I wanted to save him, but as I thought about what would happen to him if he stayed alive, I knew there was nothing I could do. I had spent almost two decades in prison, so I understood how he felt about going back. I never wanted to go back. I would rather die than do life. Like me, Trigga was a convicted felon. And he had just killed three people. Every judge in America would agree he needed to do life. So, I respected his wishes and held him while his life slowly drained out of him.

"It wasn't s'posed to happen like this. We was s'posed to kill that nigga," Trigga whispered.

"What are you talking about?" I asked, wondering if he was delirious from the blood loss.

"We was s'posed to kill Calico. Me and Luke. He gave Luke a pass, but not you. Uh!" Trigga coughed, spraying blood all over my arms.

I couldn't believe what I just heard. I felt betrayed. Luke had lied to me.

"Don't talk, Trigga. It's okay," I whispered, rubbing the top of his cornrows.

"That's my bad for lyin', Syn. I'm."

Trigga never finished his sentence. He died in my arms.

The tears that flowed down my face rushed like a river. I was hurt. And sad. Trigga was dead, and Luke had lied. As I pushed Trigga's dead body into the passenger seat, Luke's betrayal played heavily on my mind. I could have died because of his lie. And his lie had gotten Trigga killed.

J-Blunt

Chapter 27

I had just walked out of the bathroom when the front door to my apartment opened. It actually burst open. I ran to my room to get my gun. Calico had found out where I lived.

"Luke! Luke!"

I stopped in my tracks. It was Syn. Something was wrong. I could hear the alarm in her voice. I ran into the living room as fast as a running back trying to score a touchdown in the Super Bowl.

When I laid eyes upon Syn, it looked like she had been in a Texas Chainsaw Massacre movie. She was covered in blood. "Syn, what–"

"Why the fuck did you lie?" she yelled, throwing a wild punch at me.

"Hey! Chill the fuck out! What happened?" I asked, grabbing her in a bear hug.

"You got Trigga killed. You lied to me. Calico came to the studio. You lied!"

When she said Trigga was dead, it felt like someone had dropped an entire weight set on my chest. It had to be a mistake. "Where is Trigga? What are you talking about?"

"He's dead, Luke. Outside. In the car. Why did you lie? I hate–"

I let go of Syn and tore out of the apartment like I had super powers. Not my boy. Not my boy. He can't be dead.

When I got outside, I seen the town car parked in front of the building. The back window was gone. I noticed a few holes in the passenger door. Shit!

I ran toward the car looking for Trigga. I didn't see him. Not until I was all the way up on the car. He was reclined in the seat, like he was sleeping. He couldn't be dead.

"Yo, Trigga!" I yelled as I yanked open the passenger

door.

He didn't move. Didn't even flinch.

I noticed two guns on the floor mat and the blood that covered most of the interior.

He couldn't be dead.

"Yo, Trigga. Get up, nigga," I yelled, reaching down to grab him.

As soon as I touched the black t-shirt, I felt the sticky wetness. I looked down at my hands. They were covered in blood.

"Trigga, get up, fam! Get up!" I called, shaking his lifeless body. His body rocked, but he never opened his eyes.

I couldn't control the tears. They came fast and hard. It got hard for me to breathe. It felt like I was drowning. I couldn't believe my boy was dead. I had known him my whole life. He seemed invincible. Untouchable. Bullet-proof. Immortal. But now he lay lifeless in the passenger seat of a rented sedan.

My mourning was short-lived, cut off by the sound of screeching tires.

I looked up and seen a black suburban sliding to a stop in the middle of the street. Calico was in the driver's seat. A man I had never seen before came from the passenger side of the truck carrying what looked like an Uzi.

Shit!

I reached for one of the guns on the floor mat of the sedan just as the man began shooting. I wrapped my hand around the butt of one of the guns just as something slammed into my chest. I fell backwards into the grass, keeping the gun wrapped tightly in my fist.

I could feel something hot in my chest, but I ignored the pain and rolled as close to the car as I could. I had to get out of the gunman's sight.

I raised the pistol to where I thought he would come around the car at. He came into view a few moments later. I squeezed the trigger twice. Both bullets met their target, the side of the man's face.

He fell to the ground like a puppet who's strings had been snipped. I heard the suburban's engine rev and tires squeal. I jumped up and fired the rest of the bullets in the gun at the fleeing vehicle. The SUV never slowed. Calico had gotten away.

I looked back toward his slain comrade, and that's when the pain returned. It felt like someone had stuck a hot cattle prod on my chest. I looked down and seen blood soaking through my shirt.

I was shot!

I tried to run toward my building, but suddenly felt short of breath. I started coughing and spitting up blood. I tried to fight on, but couldn't. My knees got weak. and I fell onto the grass. I tried to get up, but fell to my knees again.

The inside of my chest was on fire. The worst pain I had ever felt in my life. It felt like the life was literally being drained out of me.

"Luke!"

I looked up and seen Syn running toward me. I tried to get up and go to her, but it was no use. I was too weak. I did the only thing I could do and fell into the grass face-first.

My entire life began flashing before my eyes. Christmas when I was ten. Pee-Wee football practice. High school graduation. My first day of work at the firm. The first time I laid eyes on Syn.

I wondered if this was what happened to people before they died.

To Be Continued…
A Gangster's Syn 2
Coming Soon

Submission Guideline

Submit the first three chapters of your completed manuscript to ldpsubmissions@gmail.com, subject line: Your book's title. The manuscript must be in a .doc file and sent as an attachment. Document should be in Times New Roman, double spaced and in size 12 font. Also, provide your synopsis and full contact information. If sending multiple submissions, they must each be in a separate email.

Have a story but no way to send it electronically? You can still submit to LDP/Ca$h Presents. Send in the first three chapters, written or typed, of your completed manuscript to:

LDP: Submissions Dept
Po Box 870494
Mesquite, Tx 75187

DO NOT send original manuscript. Must be a duplicate.

Provide your synopsis and a cover letter containing your full contact information.

Thanks for considering LDP and Ca$h Presents.

A Gangsta's Syn

A HUSTLER'S DECEIT 3

KILL ZONE **II**

BAE BELONGS TO ME III

SOUL OF A MONSTER

By **Aryanna**

THE COST OF LOYALTY **III**

By **Kweli**

SHE FELL IN LOVE WITH A REAL ONE **II**

By **Tamara Butler**

RENEGADE BOYS **III**

By **Meesha**

CORRUPTED BY A GANGSTA **IV**

By **Destiny Skai**

A GANGSTER'S SYN II

By **J-Blunt**

KING OF NEW YORK V

RISE TO POWER III

COKE KINGS II

By **T.J. Edwards**

GORILLAZ IN THE BAY III

De'Kari

THE STREETS ARE CALLING II

Duquie Wilson

KINGPIN KILLAZ IV

STREET KINGS 2

PAID IN BLOOD 2

Hood Rich

SINS OF A HUSTLA II
ASAD
TRIGGADALE II
Elijah R. Freeman
MARRIED TO A BOSS III
By Destiny Skai & Chris Green
KINGS OF THE GAME III
Playa Ray

<u>**Available Now**</u>
<u>RESTRAINING ORDER **I & II**</u>
By **CA$H & Coffee**
<u>LOVE KNOWS NO BOUNDARIES **I II & III**</u>
By **Coffee**
<u>RAISED AS A GOON I, II, III & IV</u>
<u>BRED BY THE SLUMS I, II, III</u>
<u>BLAST FOR ME I & II</u>
<u>ROTTEN TO THE CORE I III</u>
<u>A BRONX TALE I, II, III</u>
<u>DUFFEL BAG CARTEL I II</u>
By **Ghost**
<u>LAY IT DOWN **I & II**</u>
<u>LAST OF A DYING BREED</u>
<u>BLOOD STAINS OF A SHOTTA I & II</u>
By **Jamaica**
<u>LOYAL TO THE GAME</u>

A Gangsta's Syn

LOYAL TO THE GAME II

LOYAL TO THE GAME III

LIFE OF SIN I, II

By **TJ & Jelissa**

BLOODY COMMAS I & II

SKI MASK CARTEL I II & III

KING OF NEW YORK I II,III IV

RISE TO POWER I II

COKE KINGS

By **T.J. Edwards**

IF LOVING HIM IS WRONG…I & II

LOVE ME EVEN WHEN IT HURTS I II

By **Jelissa**

WHEN THE STREETS CLAP BACK I & II III

By **Jibril Williams**

A DISTINGUISHED THUG STOLE MY HEART I II & III

LOVE SHOULDN'T HURT I II III IV

RENEGADE BOYS I & II

By **Meesha**

A GANGSTER'S CODE I &, II III

A GANGSTER'S SYN

By J-Blunt

PUSH IT TO THE LIMIT

By **Bre' Hayes**

BLOOD OF A BOSS **I, II, III, IV, V**

By **Askari**

THE STREETS BLEED MURDER **I, II & III**

J-Blunt

THE HEART OF A GANGSTA I II& III

By **Jerry Jackson**

CUM FOR ME

CUM FOR ME 2

CUM FOR ME 3

CUM FOR ME 4

An **LDP Erotica Collaboration**

BRIDE OF A HUSTLA **I II & II**

THE FETTI GIRLS **I, II& III**

CORRUPTED BY A GANGSTA I, II & III

By **Destiny Skai**

WHEN A GOOD GIRL GOES BAD

By **Adrienne**

THE COST OF LOYALTY

By Kweli

A GANGSTER'S REVENGE **I II III & IV**

THE BOSS MAN'S DAUGHTERS

THE BOSS MAN'S DAUGHTERS II

THE BOSSMAN'S DAUGHTERS III

THE BOSSMAN'S DAUGHTERS IV

THE BOSS MAN'S DAUGHTERS **V**

A SAVAGE LOVE **I & II**

BAE BELONGS TO ME I II

A HUSTLER'S DECEIT I, II, III

WHAT BAD BITCHES DO I, II, III

By **Aryanna**

A KINGPIN'S AMBITON

232

A Gangsta's Syn

LOVE & CHASIN' PAPER

By **Qay Crockett**

TO DIE IN VAIN

SINS OF A HUSTLA

By **ASAD**

BROOKLYN HUSTLAZ

By **Boogsy Morina**

BROOKLYN ON LOCK I & II

By **Sonovia**

GANGSTA CITY

By **Teddy Duke**

A DRUG KING AND HIS DIAMOND I & II III

A DOPEMAN'S RICHES

HER MAN, MINE'S TOO I, II

CASH MONEY HO'S

By Nicole Goosby

TRAPHOUSE KING **I II & III**

KINGPIN KILLAZ I II III

STREET KINGS

PAID IN BLOOD

By **Hood Rich**

LIPSTICK KILLAH **I, II, III**

CRIME OF PASSION I & II

By **Mimi**

STEADY MOBBN' **I, II, III**

By **Marcellus Allen**

WHO SHOT YA **I, II, III**

Renta

<u>GORILLAZ IN THE BAY **I II**</u>

DE'KARI

<u>TRIGGADALE</u>

Elijah R. Freeman

<u>GOD BLESS THE TRAPPERS I, II, III</u>

<u>THESE SCANDALOUS STREETS I, II, III</u>

<u>FEAR MY GANGSTA I, II, III</u>

<u>THESE STREETS DON'T LOVE NOBODY I, II</u>

<u>BURY ME A G I, II, III, IV, V</u>

<u>A GANGSTA'S EMPIRE I, II, III</u>

Tranay Adams

<u>THE STREETS ARE CALLING</u>

Duquie Wilson

<u>MARRIED TO A BOSS… I II</u>

By Destiny Skai & Chris Green

<u>KINGS OF THE GAME I II</u>

Playa Ray

<u>BOOKS BY LDP'S CEO, CA$H</u>

<u>TRUST IN NO MAN</u>

<u>TRUST IN NO MAN 2</u>

<u>TRUST IN NO MAN 3</u>

<u>BONDED BY BLOOD</u>

<u>SHORTY GOT A THUG</u>

<u>THUGS CRY</u>

<u>THUGS CRY 2</u>

<u>THUGS CRY 3</u>

<u>TRUST NO BITCH</u>

<u>TRUST NO BITCH 2</u>

<u>TRUST NO BITCH 3</u>

<u>TIL MY CASKET DROPS</u>

<u>RESTRAINING ORDER</u>

<u>RESTRAINING ORDER 2</u>

<u>IN LOVE WITH A CONVICT</u>

<u>Coming Soon</u>

BONDED BY BLOOD 2

BOW DOWN TO MY GANGSTA

A Gangsta's Syn